DOG WHISPERER
the
RESCUE

DOG WHISPERER

the

RESCUE

By Nicholas Edwards

SQUARE
FISH

NEW YORK

A SQUARE FISH BOOK
An Imprint of Macmillan

Library of Congress Cataloging-in-Publication Data
Edwards, Nicholas.
Dog whisperer / by Nicholas Edwards.—1st ed.
p. cm.
Summary: Eleven-year-old Emily's nightmares of drowning lead
her to an injured dog near her family's coastal Maine home, and
as she nurses him back to health, she becomes aware that they
have a strange psychic connection.
ISBN: 978-0-312-36768-8
[1. Human-animal communication—Fiction.   2. Animal
rescue—Fiction.   3. Dogs—Fiction.   4. Racially mixed
people—Fiction.   5. Adoption—Fiction.   6. Family life—
Maine—Fiction.   7. Maine—Fiction.]   I. Title.
PZ7.E2634Dog 2009   [Fic]—dc22   2008040763

Design by Barbara Grzeslo
Square Fish logo designed by Filomena Tuosto

First Edition: 2009

10 9 8 7 6 5 4 3 2 1

www.squarefishbooks.com

DOG WHISPERER

the
RESCUE

1

Emily was drowning. It was very cold, and dark, and—where *was* she? The water was choppy, and deep, and seemed to be swirling around her. She tried to swim, but the current was too strong. Then, a huge wave came rushing towards her, and she felt herself being sucked under.

She fought her way back to the surface, gasping and choking and fighting for air. Okay, okay, she shouldn't panic. It would only make things worse, if she panicked. Even though she couldn't breathe, or think, or—the water was salty. Very salty. Ocean water. She was somewhere in the ocean!

She tried to yell for help, just as another wave washed over her, and she gulped a mouthful of seawater, instead. It tasted awful, and she coughed as hard as she could, trying to spit it out. The surf was so rough that it was hard to stay afloat, and she paddled frantically, trying to keep her head above water. She knew how to swim—she was *sure* she knew

1

how to swim—but, for some reason, she couldn't seem to remember any of the things she had been taught. So, she just thrashed around wildly, hoping to find a rock, or a buoy, or *anything* she could reach out and grab.

How had she gotten here? Had they been out on a sailboat? Or one of her mother's kayaks? Her parents *never* let her go in the ocean by herself, even in the daytime! There was no moon, and she couldn't see any lights, so she must be *way* far out. Alone. In the middle of the ocean. The thought of that was so scary that she screamed for help, but only managed to choke on more water. She gasped and coughed until she could breathe again, paddling frantically the entire time.

"Mom!" she shouted. "Dad! Where are you?"

But, the only thing she could hear was the pounding of the waves, and the only thing she could *see* was the pitch-black night.

She was going to drown. Right here, right now. Her arms and legs were getting weaker, and she *knew* she was going to drown. She was so tired—and scared—that she wanted to give up and let herself go under, but she decided to call for them one more time and see if they could save her before she—

"Emily," a voice was saying.

Her mother's voice. She wasn't alone! Emily twisted around in the water, trying to find her. There was too much water in her lungs for her to be able to speak, and she coughed violently, her whole body convulsing with the effort.

"Emily," her mother said, sounding gentle. "Emily, wake up."

Her mother was a *really* good swimmer, so they would be safe. Her mother would figure out some way to—"Where's the boat?" Emily gasped.

"*Wake up*, Emily," her mother said. "Everything's okay."

Emily looked around, trying to locate her in the dark water—but, it *wasn't* dark. And, suddenly, they *weren't* in the water. They were in her room, with the light on. Her mother was sitting on the edge of the bed, looking worried, and her cat, Josephine, was staring at her from on top of the dresser. Now, her father was coming into the bedroom, too, looking sleepy and confused—and very nearsighted as he fumbled to put on his glasses.

"What happened?" he asked. "What's wrong?"

"Nothing," her mother said calmly. "Emily just had a bad dream. Everything's okay now."

Her father frowned. "Another? Were you drowning again?"

Emily still felt scared and trembly, but she definitely *was* in her room, safe indoors. Not in the ocean. Not lost. Not alone. And, most important, she *wasn't* about to drown. She checked her t-shirt, which felt dry, so she must not have been anywhere *near* the water, even though the dream had seemed completely real. *Incredibly* real. "I-I think so," she said, and coughed some more, because her lungs still felt—weird. Congested.

Her father frowned again. "Three nights in a row?"

The nightmare had been a little bit different each time, but yeah, she had been having bad dreams for several days, and almost all of them were about drowning. "Is it weird to have it more than once?" she asked uneasily.

Her mother shook her head. "No, of course not. You're probably just overtired from the game."

Emily was still trying to wake up, so she wasn't sure what that meant, but then she remembered. She and her father had driven down to Portland to watch the Sea Dogs play, and the game had gone into extra innings, so they had gotten home much later than they had planned. Her father hated exercise—of all kinds, but he loved to *watch* sports. Her mother, on the other hand, was surprisingly athletic—but, did not enjoy being a spectator.

"And, you know, we ate quite a lot," her father said thoughtfully.

That was for sure. Her father had had a hot dog, a lobster roll, *and* a fish sandwich, and she'd gotten popcorn, cotton candy, some fried dough, a huge soda, and two Sea Dog Biscuits—which were ice cream sandwiches made of vanilla ice cream and chocolate chip cookies. On top of that, their team had lost, after the bullpen gave up a whole bunch of runs in the twelfth inning, which had made her feel kind of sick. Then, when they turned on the car radio on the way back home, they found out that the *Red Sox* had lost, too—which was always upsetting news, for people who lived in New England.

But, at least they had gotten bobbleheads.

"Maybe you had the nightmare because of the bullpen," her father said, and shuddered a little. "I know *I* had trouble falling asleep."

Emily's mother laughed. "Go back to bed, Theo, okay?"

While her father gave her a hug good-night,

her mother went out to the bathroom and came back with a wet washcloth. She sat back down on the edge of the bed and used the towel to sponge off Emily's face.

Cool washcloths were her mother's cure for all illnesses. "I don't think I have a fever, Mom," Emily said, although she coughed experimentally, just to make sure she wasn't sick.

Her mother shrugged. "Well, just in case."

Josephine, who was a small, round tiger cat, landed noisily on the bed. When she was younger, Emily's father had read her a poem about fog—and they had *lots* of fog in Maine—coming in on "little cat feet." That might be true, but Josephine had always been really, really *loud*. She walked loudly, ate loudly, and *purred* loudly. When Emily had pointed this out to her father, he had frowned for a minute, and then said, "Well, that just makes her the exception to prove the rule."

Anyway, Josephine sat down on the quilt, yawned a big yawn, and then began to wash her own face very delicately.

"I think she wants you to do it for her," Emily said.

Her mother shrugged. "Okay," she said, and

wiped the washcloth lightly across the top of Josephine's head.

Josephine reacted with an expression of complete cat horror, and leaped back onto the dresser to safety. That was pretty funny, and normally, Emily would have laughed, but she still felt—strange. Confused. A little bit dizzy.

"Do you think you're going to have any trouble getting back to sleep?" her mother asked.

Emily looked over at the clock, and saw that it was almost three in the morning. She knew she should be tired, but she wasn't. If anything, she felt sort of jumpy and nervous. Tense. *Alert*. Wide awake. "I don't know," she said nervously. "I'm not sure. I feel weird."

Her mother reached down to touch her forehead with the back of her hand. "Well, you don't seem to be warm."

No, she felt cold. Really cold. And scared, and lost, and alone—even though she was right here, at home, with her parents, and her cat, in her own bedroom. But she was still more scared than she had ever been in her whole life.

"Are you all right?" her mother asked.

Could she have a nightmare while she was still

awake? Because it seemed that way. She suddenly felt like she wasn't even inside of herself—and it was really, really scary.

"What's wrong?" her mother asked, looking at her attentively.

Emily shook her head. "I don't know," she said, hearing her voice shake. "I think there's something wrong with me."

Something *bad*!

2

Then, just like that, the terror went away, and Emily blinked.

"What?" her mother asked, her expression still very concerned.

"I don't know." Emily took a deep breath, and it seemed—normal. She felt normal again. Her bedroom looked the way it always did, and so did everything else. None of it made any sense, and she frowned. "I felt like I was still dreaming. Like—I don't know—I wasn't really *here*. It was creepy."

"I really think you're just overtired," her mother said. "Should we read for a while, until you're ready to go back to sleep?"

As long as she could remember, she and her parents had had a ritual of reading together, and they each took turns choosing what book they would read next. Right now, they were in the middle of a really great book full of knights and adventures and big, epic battles.

"We shouldn't really do it without Dad, though," Emily said. Because, of course, that would wreck the ritual.

"Okay." Her mother stood up. "Why don't we go downstairs and find something to eat? Or I can fix you some hot chocolate."

That seemed like a good idea, and Emily put on some socks to use as slippers. Her mother, on the other hand, was wearing *actual* slippers—which were yellow with black spots and shaped like dinosaurs—or maybe leopards; Emily had never been able to decide.

Once they were in the kitchen, Emily sat at the table, while her mother opened the refrigerator.

"What do you think you'd like?" her mother asked, rummaging around inside. Her mother wasn't crazy about cooking, but she enjoyed it more than Emily's father, who was from Manhattan and always wanted to get take-out. "Yogurt, maybe? Or I could heat up some of the macaroni and cheese?"

Emily tipped back in her chair—which she *completely* wasn't supposed to do—so that she could see inside. A bunch of blueberries and raspberries, which they had picked at her parents' friends' farm, what looked like lobster salad—yuck, what was left of a roast chicken her father had brought home from the deli, chocolate pudding cups, eggs, lots of milk and juice, some iced tea her mother always made by putting a big glass jar out on the deck on sunny days, a plastic container of tofu and carrot casserole, and lots of other stuff. *Healthy* stuff. Boring stuff.

"Please don't do that," her mother said sharply. "I don't want you to fall."

Emily shifted her weight so that all four chair legs were back on the floor again. "Could I have a drumstick, please?"

Her mother looked startled. "What?"

Emily pointed at the small roast chicken.

"Oh." Her mother gave her a strange look, but took the package out and put it on the counter. "Sure. Okay. Would you like a sandwich, or—"

"Just the drumstick, please," Emily said. "I mean, unless Dad was, like, saving it, or something."

Her mother shook her head, carefully twisted the drumstick off, and then put it on one of the hand-glazed clay plates her friend Tanya, who was an art history professor, had made. "How about some toast, too?"

Emily nodded, feeling more and more hungry. Starving, in fact. She had thought that she would be stuffed for a *week*, after all the food she had eaten at the baseball game, but it turned out that she had only been full for about three hours.

But, when her mother set the plate in front of her, Emily frowned down at the drumstick. It looked sort of *disgusting*. Crisp brown skin, dark meat, *bone*—it was really gross. Why had she asked if she could have it?

Her mother was just standing there, watching her. "You don't want that at all, do you?" she asked.

Not even a little bit. Emily shook her head.

"I didn't think so." Her mother took the plate away, moved the toast to a clean plate, and spread some peanut butter on the bread before handing it to her.

Emily could have sworn that she wanted some chicken—*craved* it, in fact—but that was totally weird, because she didn't eat meat anymore. *Ever*. Not even bacon, although she had to admit that it sometimes actually smelled pretty good. She had made up her mind that she wanted to be a vegetarian back when she was about nine, because eating animals just seemed—wrong. In fact, she had also decided that she wanted to be a veterinarian when she grew up, so she could spend her life *helping* animals.

Actually, she loved to draw, so she kind of wanted

to be an artist, too—but, maybe it would be possible to do *both*.

Her parents didn't like the idea of her not eating meat, because they said she was still growing and needed the protein. But, in the end, her mother had talked to Emily's pediatrician, and then went out and bought about a million vegetarian cookbooks. She had also gone over to Dining Services at the college—her parents were both professors at Bowdoin—to discuss healthy menus they could prepare. On top of that, she had even made an appointment with a nutritionist, and all three of them had gone and sat for an hour and a half with a really tall lady who gave them lots of pamphlets and sample diets and everything. That same night, her father had carefully hung a poster of the vegetarian food pyramid on the wall near the pantry, and both of her parents still consulted it for a couple of minutes almost every time one of them prepared a meal for her.

Her mother sat down across from her with a glass of iced tea. "You know, you don't *always* have to be a vegetarian, if you don't want to be. You're allowed to change your—"

"No, I still want to do it," Emily said quickly. "I guess I just forgot."

Her mother nodded. "Okay. But, maybe we should talk about it with Dr. Socoby next week."

School was going to be starting soon, so she had to go for a full check-up, and get weighed and everything. Emily looked at her anxiously. "Do you think something's wrong with me? Because I've been having bad dreams and all?"

"Of course not," her mother said. "I think you're probably just nervous about junior high. It's perfectly normal."

Well, she definitely *was* nervous about having to go to a new school. Most of the other sixth graders from her elementary school would be there, too, but the junior high was much bigger, and there would be lots of people she didn't know. And she would have all new teachers, some of whom might not be nice. Like in kindergarten, when her teacher met her, she had immediately asked if she might need remedial tutoring—even though Emily had been reading chapter books for almost a year by then. Her parents got *really* mad, and had her switched to the other class right away.

She glanced at her mother. "Do you and Dad have nightmares?"

"Sure," her mother said, with a shrug. "Sometimes. Everyone does."

But probably not three days in a row. "It could, um, maybe be genetic," Emily said, avoiding her mother's eyes. "Having lots of bad dreams."

"Well—" Her mother hesitated. "Yes. I suppose it could be."

Her parents were *her parents*, and she almost never thought about being adopted—except that sometimes, she did. And they didn't talk much about the fact that she was biracial, and her parents—weren't. Her mother had blond hair, even. Well, greyish blond, but still blond. It totally didn't matter, and it was mostly just funny, like when her father got all into celebrating Kwanzaa and everything, and she had had to make him promise *never* to wear kente cloth in front of her friends again. She had also told him that if he ever showed up in a dashiki, she was going to run away and join the circus—or maybe get a job working for a hedge fund. Her mother had laughed, but her father had just seemed disappointed about having to limit his holiday celebration.

"Do you have questions?" her mother asked, her expression very serious. "Would you like to talk about it?"

Yes—and no. Emily thought it over, and then shook her head.

"We can *always* talk about it," her mother said

earnestly. "Whenever you want. Especially if anything is bothering you."

Lots of times, it felt like her parents were more comfortable talking about it than *she* was. Emily shook her head. "No, I don't really want to right now. I mean, thank you, but—no. I just—think about them, sometimes." Her birth parents. Whoever they were. *Wherever* they were.

Her mother started to say something, but then just nodded and sipped her tea, while Emily ate her peanut butter toast. They stayed up for a while longer and talked about what kind of new clothes she was going to need for school, and whether it was possible to watch too many movies starring Julie Andrews, and other relaxing things like that.

But Emily was starting to get very sleepy, and they went upstairs so that they could both go back to bed. After she brushed her teeth, they discussed whether she was too old to be tucked in. Emily definitely thought she was, but always let her mother do it, anyway, because she knew it made her happy.

Her mother kissed her good-night. "Sleep well. And don't turn the light back on and read all night!"

Emily grinned sheepishly, since sometimes she did that, and ended up falling asleep with the light on. Then, whichever parent came in to wake her up the next morning would know that she had stayed awake reading when she was supposed to be asleep.

Tonight, though, she was really tired. Josephine curled up next to her, purring enthusiastically, and Emily patted her until she finally dropped off to sleep.

Then, it was later—she wasn't sure how *much* later—and it was cold, and there was water everywhere, and she couldn't breathe, and—

She was drowning again!

3

This time, part of her knew that it really was only a dream, but she still *felt* as though she was drowning. The waves seemed bigger than ever, and there were rocks around, too, because she kept crashing into them— which *hurt*. It seemed to take forever, but finally, she managed to wake herself up. She pulled her quilt closer, shivering and scared. Water seemed to be pouring all over the place, and at first, she was very confused. Then, she realized that it was raining outside.

Rain wasn't scary. She had probably just had the dream again because of the sound of it pounding against the roof.

It seemed to be very windy—her shade and curtains were flapping back and forth. A big storm must have whipped in off the bay, because it sounded really wild outside. Lots of times, her mother liked to go for walks during storms, but Emily and her father would usually just say, "Yeah, okay, whatever, have fun," and stay in and eat cookies and read by the fire-place.

Actually, no, they would *start* by reading—or Emily would sit in the big, blue easy chair and draw. Since her parents were both academics, they spent *a lot* of time reading and doing research. But Emily could almost always talk her father into playing a couple of Wii games, instead. They would jump around, and make a lot of commotion—and because her father was pretty uncoordinated, he would generally knock over a lamp or some candlesticks or something. Her mother didn't really approve of video games, but whenever they got her to give the Wii a try, she would get hooked and play for about two hours straight.

The rain was coming down even harder now, and she was glad she was indoors. The shade and curtains looked like they were doing a weird shadow dance together, which was kind of cool—but, maybe a little creepy, too.

Emily wanted to stay under the covers, but the wind was pretty cold. Besides, some rain might blow in and get on her computer, and *that* would be bad. So, she dragged herself up and over to the window. There wasn't any lightning, but she could hear cracking sounds as tree branches broke. Every so often, a foghorn blared out, too, and she hoped no boats were caught in the storm. They knew lots of people in Bailey's Cove who fished for a living or were lobstermen—including her friend Bobby's father—and it would be really dangerous if any of them were out there.

It took some effort, because the wind was so strong, but she finally managed to pull the window shut.

"Wow," she said to Josephine. "That's a really big—" She stopped when she saw that her cat was suddenly standing absolutely upright on the bed, with her fur all ruffled up. "Hey, what is it?"

Josephine just stared past her, looking alert and alarmed, with her tail straight up in the air.

Maybe there was a seagull or something out there? Whatever it was had her cat's full attention!

Mostly, though, Josephine wasn't that interested in birds. Or squirrels or raccoons or deer—or even the seals that they sometimes found lying happily on the rocks by the water, getting some sun. Personally, Emily thought the seals were really cool. Once, a moose had even shown up in their backyard—and pretty much trampled all over the garden. But Josephine usually just liked to yawn a lot, take long naps, have some food, and then go sleep some more. So there had to be something really unusual out there, if she was actually *interested*.

It probably wasn't a bear, or a bobcat, or anything like that, because they didn't really come down to the south coast—but, wow, what if it *was*? That would be pretty neat. Her father always said that he didn't like nature at all, but he was really into photography—almost always *film*, not digital—and they had lots of framed pictures of loons and deer and stuff around the house.

Josephine jumped over to the windowsill and began to pace back and forth, with her tail whipping from side to side.

Okay, there definitely *was* something out there. But her cat didn't seem nervous; she seemed uneasy. Anxious. *Worried*.

Emily squinted out at the storm, but it was too foggy to be able to see anything.

"Whatever it is," she said to her cat, "it'll probably go away."

As she turned to go to bed, Josephine meowed so loudly that Emily turned back.

"What?" she asked, a little bit impatiently. Even if there was some wild animal lurking around, it wasn't like she was going to go charging out there to—then, she stopped.

Was something—crying for help? She didn't think she could hear anything over the rain, but it *felt* as though—Emily frowned.

It didn't make sense, but all of a sudden, she was completely convinced that there was something out there that needed her!

Her parents probably had a rule that she wasn't supposed to go running around outside at the crack of dawn in the middle of a summer squall—but, it had actually never come up before. So, Emily decided not to worry about it. Besides, she was only going to be in the *backyard*. After already waking them up earlier, she really didn't want to do it again.

She had worn a pair of green shorts and a Yarmouth Clam Festival t-shirt to bed, so all she needed was some sneakers and a hoodie. She started out of her bedroom, then went back and swapped her sneakers for her L.L. Bean boots.

It was raining even harder than she expected, and she should have put on her slicker, first. But she was *already* soaked now, so it probably didn't matter. Even though it was light out, now, it was really, really foggy, and she couldn't really see the soft glow of the lighthouse up on the point. But, she could hear its foghorn, as well as the one way up at Halfway Rock.

Their town was a long peninsula, with a couple of islands, which were connected to the rest of the town by bridges. Her family's house was right on the water and had a tiny floating dock. Her mother went kayaking almost every morning, and she would paddle for a couple of miles up and down the sound. They also had an old wooden skiff, which they usually kept upside down on the lawn, because the shoreline was all rocks, with no sandy places.

They had neighbors on both sides—and all along the peninsula—but their yard had lots of trees, so it always felt really private. The trees meant that they didn't get much sun, but her parents had had a wooden deck built, anyway. Sometimes, they had supper out there, at a picnic table. Lots of nights, they would hang out on the deck until after dark— unless the black flies got so annoying that they would have to go indoors to escape them.

It was so difficult to see through the rain and fog, that she stood on the deck and listened, instead. Wind, rain, waves crashing against the rocks.

Maybe Josephine had just been acting weird, and there wasn't anything out here at all.

Maybe.

The lawn sloped downhill to the rocks, and the grass was so wet that she was really glad she'd changed into her boots. There were a few branches strewn around, but other than that, everything seemed to be normal. She turned around to check every direction but didn't see anything other than grass, a few bushes, and their garden—where her mother and grandmother had planted tomatoes, zucchini, and some flowers. So far, though, mostly only the weeds were thriving.

There was a low rumble of thunder, and she immediately decided to go back indoors. Besides, she was really tired.

She was halfway back to the house, when she felt—well—*something*. She felt afraid, or anxious, or—urgent. Yeah, she definitely felt this strange sense of needing to take action. *Immediately*.

But, doing *what*?

Maybe her father was right, and she had just eaten way too much food at the baseball game, and now she had, like, indigestion. Which would make more sense if her stomach hurt—but, it didn't.

There was a flash of lightning, and then more thunder, coming from the direction of the harbor, and she ducked instinctively. Okay, she would just check the yard one more time, really fast, and then go back to bed.

She walked down to the edge of the grass,

above the rocks, and towards one of their neighbors' houses.

She squinted through the fog, but all that she could see was crashing waves and rocks. Lots of rocks. The Peabodys' dinghy, tied to their dock, and bobbing up and down in the choppy water. A few lobster buoys. Other than that, she couldn't find anything unusual, or—wait!

There *was* something out there!

Emily looked more closely, and realized that there was a large, white shape on the rocks. Was it an old sail, maybe? Or a piece of plastic, or some Styrofoam? But, the shape seemed to be too big for that. What it looked like was an animal of some kind. In fact, it *looked* like a polar bear.

Whoa. She was almost a thousand percent sure that there were no polar bears in Maine—but what if one had gotten lost, and drifted down from— what, the North Pole? No, that was just silly. It was probably only some junk that had washed up onto the rocks because of the storm.

She took a few cautious steps towards the bulky shape.

Was there such a thing as an albino seal? Whales sometimes beached themselves, and this might be a poor baby whale that had floundered into the cove and was too weak to swim anymore. Or even a shark, or a porpoise or something. When the surf was high, all kinds of fish and marine mammals showed up unexpectedly. The coast of Maine was so rocky and uneven, with lots of islands and inlets and coves and all, that it was probably really easy for animals to get lost.

But, if it was a baby whale or something, it wouldn't be able to breathe much longer, if it couldn't get back into the water. Anyone who found a beached animal was supposed to call the authorities right away so that they could come out and help save it. Emily wasn't quite sure exactly *who* to call, but her mother would know, because she did, like, advisory work for the state senate president when the legislature was in session and worked on environmental issues and all.

More worried than afraid now, she walked closer. There were a few thick bushes in the way, and a wet branch smacked her in the face.

"Ow," she said automatically.

She tried to squeeze her way through the branches, but the bushes were too dense. They *were* tall enough so that maybe she could crawl underneath them, instead. She crouched down, buried almost to her ankles in the mud. It was going to be messy to crawl through all of that! And she *liked* this shirt.

But, she stretched out onto her stomach and squirmed through to the other side, anyway. The mud felt really cold and gross, and she wiped as much of it off as she could with her free hand.

Now, she could see that it was definitely an animal out there. A coyote, maybe? She was always extra careful to make sure that Josephine stayed inside, because there were coyote sightings all the time.

It might be dangerous to go right up next to it and check, but whatever the animal was, it seemed to be hurt. She needed to find out, one way or the other.

Without thinking, she whistled a low, sharp whistle—and the animal immediately lifted its head and looked in her direction.

Hey, it wasn't a coyote; it was a *dog*! A big, white, soaking wet dog. A retriever, maybe.

"Here, boy!" she called. "Come here, boy!"

The dog tried to move, but then slumped back down.

She wasn't sure if he was just tired, or injured, but there was obviously something wrong with him.

"Come on, boy," she said encouragingly. "You can do it."

The dog struggled to get up, then whimpered

and fell heavily onto his side. He whimpered again, and then lay still.

Maybe he was caught on something, like rope, or an old fishing net, and because of that, he was trapped. She was going to have to go out there and help him.

The rocks were very slippery, and it was going to be that much harder to keep her balance in the pouring rain. Emily hesitated, but slowly began to make her way towards the dog. If she got her ankle caught in a crevice, or fell into the water or something, she wasn't going to be much help. And with no one around to rescue her, she wouldn't be able to rescue *him*—which meant that they would both be in big trouble.

Lightning flashed, followed by another crash of thunder a few seconds later. The dog cringed—and so did she.

"Good dog," she said, trying to sound brave. "Everything's okay."

She tried to avoid the rocks with too much algae, but kept slipping anyway. Her boots didn't seem to have any traction, and suddenly, her legs slid out from underneath her and she banged her right knee so hard that she gasped. In fact, it hurt so much that she almost started crying, but she just stayed where she was, taking a few deep breaths to try and make the pain go away.

Okay, falling *that* heavily had maybe not been part of her plan.

"Um, sorry, I hurt my leg a little," she said to the dog, as she pushed herself back up to her feet. "I'm okay, though. Just hang tight, I'm coming." Not that she was expecting the dog to *answer*—but it seemed polite.

The rocks were so treacherous and slick that she decided to be smart and take her time. She would lift one boot, set it down cautiously, make sure she was well anchored, and then brace herself with her hands before moving her other foot forward. It wasn't fast, but it was *safe*.

Well, *kind* of safe. In bright sunlight, when she could see what she was doing, and it wasn't raining like crazy, with lightning and thunder and fog everywhere.

Okay, it wasn't *at all* safe. And her knee hurt—a lot. But she still didn't stop, moving slowly and steadily towards him.

She was so close now that she could hear the dog panting, although it sounded more like wheezing. When the next flash of lightning came, she could see some dark splotches on his fur, so maybe he was white with black spots. The only thing she could tell for sure was that he was *big*. Maybe ninety or a hundred pounds.

"Hey, boy," she said, in a nice, calm voice. She had never had her own dog before—although she had always wanted one—but she had been taught to be very careful around animals she didn't know. Her parents had said that it was even more important when it was a stray animal who might be scared, and would maybe snap at her out of pure panic and fear.

"Good boy," she said, even more calmly.

The dog was obviously very weak and in a lot of pain, but he raised his tail enough to wag it once.

Between the rain and ocean spray, it was getting even harder to keep her footing, but finally, she was close enough to touch him. She reached out to pat his head, and he licked her hand, his tongue feeling very dry.

"Good dog," she said. "You're a good boy."

Another huge wave came crashing up onto the rocks, and she lifted her arm to try and block both of them from the spray. It worked pretty well, but a second wave rushed in a few seconds later, and they both got even more drenched than they already were.

"I'm sorry," she said. "I didn't see that one coming."

The dog's tail thumped, faintly.

What she needed now was a plan. The first thing she had to do was to move the dog off the rocks, and away from the surging water.

"Can you get up?" she asked, and snapped her fingers reflexively. "Come on, you can do it."

The dog just lay there, his breathing raspy and uneven.

"Come on, boy," she said encouragingly.

He still didn't move.

Okay, he was way too big for her to pick up, but maybe she could try to pull him, a little bit, if she was very gentle. She reached out, feeling for a collar, but there didn't seem to be anything around his neck. So, she decided to see if she could help him stand up, instead.

But, when she touched his front leg, he yelped so loudly that she dodged away from him—and almost fell off the rocks into the churning water.

"I'm sorry," she said quickly. "I didn't mean to do that. I'm really sorry."

The dog moved his head towards her, and she was a little afraid that he might bite her, but he just licked her hand again. He was shivering badly, and she rested her hand lightly on his head, not sure what else to do.

It seemed to be raining harder than ever, and she wasn't quite sure what to do.

"It's going to be okay," she said. "It really is."

The dog just lay on his side, gasping for air.

She needed to go get some help.

Fast.

5

"**I**'ll be right back," she said. "I promise."

Would it be okay to leave him for a few minutes? What if more big waves came in, and the current pulled him off the rocks? But there was no way she could rescue him by herself. He was just too big for her to lift.

She pulled off her hoodie, and carefully covered him with it. It might not help much, but maybe it would keep him a *little* warmer while she ran back to the house.

"*Stay*," she said. "Good dog. Stay."

She scrambled over the rocks, through the bushes, across the lawn, and up onto the deck. Then, she yanked the back door open and ran upstairs to her parents' bedroom.

Since her mother had stayed up so late and was probably really tired, she decided to try and wake up her father, instead. Besides, her mother was really small—Emily was already almost as tall as she was—so her father would have an easier time picking the dog up.

"Dad?" she whispered.

It took three tries, but finally, he opened his eyes, looking confused.

"What?" he asked, and blinked a few times. "What is it?" He rubbed one hand across his eyes. "Did you have another dream?"

"There's a *dog*," Emily said.

Her father looked puzzled, and hoisted himself up onto one elbow. "You dreamed about a dog?"

Emily shook her head. "No, it's a *real* dog. Out on the rocks. He needs a vet."

Her father glanced over his shoulder to make sure her mother was still asleep. "What do you mean?" he asked quietly. "I don't understand."

"I found a dog," Emily said. "But it's a really *big* dog, and I can't get him inside by myself."

Her father must still have been half-asleep, because his expression was entirely befuddled. "Why are you all wet?"

"It's raining," she said. "Please, Dad? I need your help."

That must have been the magic word, because now her mother woke up, too.

"What's wrong?" she asked sleepily.

By the time Emily had explained the whole thing again, her father had pulled on a pair of hiking boots and put on a Bowdoin sweatshirt over his pajamas.

"You want me to come out with you?" Emily's mother asked, already lacing up a pair of running shoes.

Her father shook his head. "No, don't worry, Joanne, I'll take care of it. It'll only take a couple of minutes."

Once they were outside, Emily hurried across the lawn, towards the Peabodys' house.

"It's *pouring* out here," her father said. "Go in and get your jacket."

She shook her head. "It's okay, Dad, I'm already wet."

Her father's sigh was either long-suffering—or kind of annoyed.

"I promise I'll get one after," she said.

Her father clearly didn't see the logic of that, but he nodded, in a *distinctly* long-suffering way.

She veered around a familiar long object on the ground, and then remembered how clumsy her father was even when—unlike now—he was wide awake. Emily turned to head him off. "Dad, don't fall over the—"

Her father tripped, and went sprawling.

Too late. "Um, kayak," she said. Her mother kept her good racing kayak in the garage, but often left her everyday one outside, carefully protected by a thick, waterproof cover.

"Did I break the rudder again?" he asked, from the muddy ground.

Boy, she sure hoped not, because her mother had been pretty mad the other two times it happened. "I think it's okay," she said uncertainly.

"Let's *hope* it's okay," he said.

When they got to the Peabodys' bushes, her father frowned, stumbling slightly on the rough ground. "This is pretty far from the house, Emily."

She had kind of been hoping that he wouldn't notice that part, since she might get in trouble for running around by herself in the middle of a storm this early in the morning. "I could *hear* him," Emily said. Sort of. "Josephine was acting all weird, and, like, banging at the window with her paws."

"Hmmm," her father said. "That *is* weird."

The rain was coming down harder than ever, but at least, the thunderstorm seemed to be moving out to sea, because the lightning flashes were less frequent, and the thunder sounded farther away.

Emily started to climb underneath the bushes, but her father pulled her back.

"Why don't we just go up this way, Em?" he suggested, pointing towards the Peabodys' driveway.

Well—yeah, that made kind of a lot of sense. Emily nodded, and followed him across the yard, up to the road, and then down the driveway.

"Why are you limping?" her father asked.

Because her knee hurt. "I'm fine," Emily said, and made a point of *not* limping.

They hurried past the bushes—her father tripping again, and snapping off a few small branches—and towards the rocks.

When she saw the big white shape still lying there, she let out a sigh of relief.

"See?" She pointed, and started making her way across the rocks. "Right over there."

Her father followed her, slipping several times. "You didn't climb out here by yourself, did you?" he asked.

Emily had never been good at lying—and it wasn't something she liked to do, anyway. "The dog was *crying*, Dad."

And now that they were closer, she could hear that the dog *was* whimpering a little. He was on his side in the exact same spot where she had left him, his breathing labored. But, when he saw her, his tail made a feeble wag.

"You stay here, okay?" her father said. "And stand *way* back, in case he bites."

Emily shook her head. "He's not going to bite, Dad. He's a really good dog."

"Just stand back, please," her father said, hesitated for a second—he wasn't really comfortable around animals, even Josephine—and then bent down to look at the dog.

To her horror, Emily saw that the dog's fur wasn't just soaked from the ocean—there was *blood*, too, on his side, and his head and paws.

"Okay," her father said, sounding as though he was talking to himself. "Let me just figure out how to—okay." He moved, cautiously, to lift the dog up, but the dog immediately yelped from pain.

Emily swallowed, because she knew it wouldn't help if she started crying, too. "Can we call an ambulance, maybe?"

Her father thought about that, and then shook his head. "No, let me try again. I'll be more careful."

This time, the dog whimpered, but he also let out a low growl.

"Hey!" her father said, and jumped back out of the way. "Don't come anywhere near him, okay, Em?"

"I think his chest hurts a lot," Emily said, and

climbed down to pat the dog's head. "Good boy. It's okay, boy."

Her father glared at her. "What did I just tell you?"

Not to do exactly what she had immediately done. "Dad's just trying to help you," she said to the dog.

The dog's tail waved once, only lifting a couple of inches off the rocks.

"Don't touch him," her father said, his voice stern. "I don't want you to get bitten."

Emily looked at the dog, who looked back at her with distinct, expressive dark eyes. "He won't," she said. "He was just scared."

Her father frowned at her. "Emily, when I tell you to do something this important, you need to listen to me."

It didn't seem like it would be smart to argue with him, so Emily nodded and moved a few feet away.

"Thank you," her father said, and then shook his head. "I think we should probably call the police. Maybe they can—"

Emily stared at him. "The *police*?"

Her father sighed. "They know how to do this sort of thing. I'm really not—look out!"

They both ducked as a gigantic wave came

sweeping in over the rocks, washing over all three of them.

"Wow," her father said, and wiped his hand across his glasses. "That was a pretty big one."

But not as big as the *next* wave, which was strong enough to knock Emily down, and her father almost toppled over, too.

"Are you all right?" her father asked, as he helped her up. "Go back and wait on the grass, okay?"

Emily nodded, and looked down at the dog, to make sure that he was all right.

But the rocks were now empty, except for her crumpled sweatshirt.

The dog was gone!

Emily and her father stared at each other, and then out at the rough water. Her father saw him first, pointing when he located a white, bobbing shape.

"Okay, there he is," he said. "Maybe we can use a stick, or borrow some rope from the Peabodys' dock."

That made sense, but the dog was too exhausted to swim, and she saw his head go under.

"We don't have time for that, Dad," she said, and scrambled over to the edge of the rocks.

"Emily," her father said, "don't even *think* of jumping into—"

Emily jumped into the water. And wow, it was cold! *Freezing*. So cold that it took her breath away, as the shock ran through her whole body. She treaded water for a few seconds, to try and get her bearings, and then swam towards the dog in a fast, determined crawl.

Then, there was another big splash, as her father

took off his glasses, set them down on a rock, and then leaped in after her.

"I am *not* happy with you, Emily," he said grimly, as he swam ineptly in her direction.

Okay, but she had started taking swimming lessons when she was about five years old, and she was a much better swimmer than he was. Maybe she usually didn't swim during the middle of driving rainstorms, but she knew *how*.

And maybe she should have asked her mother to help with this, instead, because there was a chance she was going to have to rescue her *father*, too.

The dog was nowhere in sight, and she dove under where she had last seen him. It took three tries, as she flailed around with her arms, but finally, one of her hands grazed wet fur. He was in too much trouble for her to worry about hurting him, so she tugged as hard as she could on his legs to pull him up to the surface.

Working together, she and her father hauled him back to the rocks. The dog's body was limp, which made it easier to drag him, but she was terrified that he might be dead.

They hoisted him up onto the rocks, and then her father lifted her out of the water, too.

"Do not," he said, coughing, "*ever* do that again. I'm very cross with you."

She was coughing too much herself to be able to answer, but she nodded.

In the meantime, the dog was sprawled across the rocks, still not moving. Her father pulled himself out of the water and then looked around blearily.

His glasses. Emily glanced around until she saw them wedged in between two rocks. "Right there," she said, and picked them up for him. It looked like the frames were kind of bent, but at least they weren't broken.

Her father nodded, wiped the lenses off on his wet sweatshirt, and put the glasses on, still coughing. He frowned down at the dog, and rested his hand against his chin as he thought for a moment. Then he nodded once, and positioned the dog's head so that it was angled down.

"What are you doing?" Emily asked.

"I'm going to try some CPR," her father said, and pressed firmly on the dog's rib cage with both hands. He counted aloud to three, then pressed again—and again, and again, with the same rhythm.

Just as he bent down to breathe into the dog's mouth and nose, the dog unexpectedly choked and water gushed out of his mouth. Her father waited until he was finished, and then resumed the chest compressions.

The dog vomited up some more water—and then, it seemed like magic as his chest started moving up and down.

He was breathing on his own!

Emily was so relieved that she wasn't sure whether to hug her father or the dog—or *both*. "Wow, that was really good, Dad."

Her father just sat down on the rocks to catch his own breath.

The dog lay stoically on his side, but his breathing was more labored than ever.

"Let's get him into the house," her father said. "Then, we can decide what to do from there."

Emily nodded. The swimming had been surprisingly exhausting, and she was shivering from the chilly rain. But she picked up her sweatshirt, wrung out the water as well as she could, and covered the dog with it again.

The dog moved slightly in response, and then lay quietly again.

"Theo? Emily?" her mother called from their deck. "Where are you?"

"Over here!" her father called back.

Once her mother had made her way over to

them, her parents decided—actually, her *mother* decided—that her father would go get a couple of blankets and one of their plastic sleds. The idea was that they would ease the dog onto the sled, and then pull him safely back to the house.

Emily thought that sounded like a good plan. A *smart* plan.

She and her mother stayed on the rocks to wait for him to come back. Emily patted the dog gently the entire time.

"Dad gave him CPR," she said. "It was cool."

Her mother looked impressed. "Good for him. I don't think I'd know how to give CPR to a dog."

Emily nodded, since she wouldn't have had any idea how to do it, either. But her father had a really, really good memory, and it was the kind of thing he must have read about on the Internet once.

"Was the dog wearing that sweatshirt when you got here?" her mother asked wryly.

Emily shook her head. "No, I was trying to keep the rain from getting on him."

"Joke," her mother said.

Right. Okay. She maybe should have figured that out on her own, although it would probably have been easier if she was less tired.

She kept saying soothing things to the dog, and

every so often, he would wag his tail a tiny bit. She knew that he probably couldn't understand her, but it seemed important to try and make him feel safe.

"I know it hurts, but you should try not to growl again," she said. "Dogs make my father a little nervous."

Her mother laughed. "*A lot* of things make your father a little nervous."

Which was true. Sometimes, even ordinary stuff like the sound of blenders made him flinch. He always said that it was because he had grown up directly underneath a roller coaster, although that was actually a joke from an old movie. Anyway, he had grown up on the Upper West Side in New York in a very large apartment building, where her grandparents still lived. Her mother, on the other hand, was from Southern California and had spent most of her childhood on the beach—or playing sports with her three big brothers. Two of her brothers had even grown up to be *coaches*—her other brother was a ski instructor—and they all thought it was fairly hilarious that their little sister had gone off and gotten a PhD in history, and spent most of her time sitting behind a desk all day.

When her father returned with the sled and two blankets, he was also carrying a pair of oven mitts.

"Are your hands cold?" Emily asked dubiously.

Her father flushed slightly. "In case he snaps when we move him."

Oven mitts would probably be more protective than ordinary pot holders, but just barely.

"Hockey gloves might have been better," her mother said.

"Oh." Her father gave that some thought. "That's true."

Except that they didn't even own any hockey gloves, as far as Emily knew. They *watched* hockey sometimes, but none of them played.

Her mother folded one of the blankets in half, and spread it onto the rocks right next to the dog. Before her father could even put the oven mitts on, the dog made a sound like a resigned sigh and painfully dragged himself onto the blanket, even though his legs didn't seem to be working quite right. Then, he collapsed, breathing harder than ever.

"Wow," Emily said, feeling very proud of him. "He's really *smart*." And brave, too!

Her parents each lifted one end of the blanket, and slowly transferred the dog onto the sled. The other blanket was already pretty soaked from the rain, but her mother covered him with it, anyway, to protect him a little during the journey over to their house.

The dog was gasping for breath, but other than that, he never moved or made a sound as her father pulled the sled across the wet grass. Emily held the back door open, and her father guided the sled into the kitchen.

In the bright light of the room, she saw the dog clearly for the first time. He *was* a white retriever of some kind, with big brown eyes, and a black nose. He was so thin that all of his ribs showed, and she gasped when she saw a long bloody gash running across his side.

His left foreleg was also covered with blood and hanging in an unnatural position. When she looked more closely, she felt completely sick to her stomach.

There was a broken *bone* sticking right out of his leg!

7

"What do we do?" Emily asked, feeling panicky.

"Go get as much gauze as you can find," her mother said. "We'll just try to protect it, until we can get him to the vet."

Emily raced upstairs and grabbed all of the first-aid supplies she could find in the medicine cabinet. She handed them to her mother, who gently spread some layers of gauze over the wounds. Then, she covered him with a thick, dry beach towel.

The dog stayed on his side, shivering and panting. His chest was moving raggedly up and down, and Emily saw her parents exchange uneasy glances. She looked up at the kitchen clock, and saw that it was just past six-thirty.

"How soon can we call Dr. K.?" she asked. Dr. K.—short for Kasanofsky—was their veterinarian.

Her mother frowned, and also checked the clock. "Not for an hour or so at least, I don't think. It's awfully early."

"Can we take him to a regular hospital, instead? You know, for *people*?" Emily asked. "Right away?"

Her father shook his head. "I'm sorry, I don't think they would let us bring him into the ER. Let me go send Dr. K. an email now, though, in case he checks it before he goes to the office, and wants to call us. I'll see if I can find a twenty-four-hour clinic in Portland or someplace, too."

It was awful just to sit and watch the dog struggle to breathe, without being able to help. He was still trembling from the cold—and probably shock, too—so her mother spread another towel on top of him.

"Why don't you go get the heating pad," she suggested. "And then, we'll put it between the towels so he can warm up a little more."

Emily was happy to have a specific task. It took a couple of minutes, but she found their heating pad up in the linen closet and brought it downstairs.

Her mother set it up as delicately as she could, but the dog still whimpered a little just from having the towels adjusted on top of him. Then, he settled down and resumed the loud, raspy breathing.

"Should I give him some water?" Emily asked.

Her mother shook her head. "We can't be sure that he isn't bleeding internally. Maybe just a little."

Emily filled a small metal mixing bowl with water and carried it over.

"No, wait," her mother said quickly. "I'll give it to him."

She knew the dog wasn't going to bite—*knew* it, deep in her bones—but she cooperatively handed the bowl to her mother.

Her mother carefully set the bowl next to the dog's muzzle, and he wagged his tail once, but didn't lift his head.

"Maybe with, like, a turkey baster?" Emily asked. Did they own a turkey baster? "Or an eyedropper or something?"

"In a little while, we can try that," her mother said, and went into the pantry to get a can of beef stock. "Or maybe we should start him with some warm broth. I don't think we should do anything more than that, though, until we can get him to the vet."

It seemed to be taking him forever to come back, but she assumed that her father was doing some quick research on the Internet about how to take care of injured pets, and all of the important steps to take. He was probably already printing out pages of instructions and advice.

Ever since she was little, Emily had always read

lots of books about animals. One thing she had learned was that they sometimes knew and understood things that people didn't. That most animals were naturally *wise*. She wasn't sure if everything she had read was true, but it was all really interesting.

What she sensed from the dog right now was that he wanted to stay very, very still, and conserve his energy. So she sat quietly, too, right next to him, cross-legged on the floor, with her hands folded in her lap.

"Why don't you go upstairs and put on something dry," her mother said.

Emily looked down and realized that her clothes were dripping so much water that she was now sitting in a puddle. She went up to her room and changed into sweatpants, a pink turtleneck, thick wool socks, and sneakers. She hadn't realized how cold she had gotten from jumping into the ocean, and being out in the rain for so long—and it turned out that her knee was pretty badly bruised, too. She couldn't even *imagine* how cold the dog must be feeling.

Josephine followed her downstairs, and stopped dead in her tracks when she saw the dog lying on the floor. Emily would have expected her to hiss and tear out of the room, but she took several tentative steps in his direction. Then, she sniffed at the towels covering him, sniffed at his muzzle—and tore out of the room.

"Here," Emily's mother said, and handed her a mug of hot chocolate.

Emily was still cold and accepted it gratefully. "Thank you," she said, and sat back down on the floor next to the dog.

Her mother had already heated some broth, and Emily held the bowl close to the dog's nose so that he could smell it. He actually cocked one of his ears, and looked alert for the first time. So she moved the bowl to a more comfortable angle, and he drank a little—and spilled even more. Then, he must have gotten tired, because he sighed, and let his head slump down again.

"I wish he had a collar," her mother said. "Then, we could call his owners and let them know that we found him."

Emily hadn't even considered the fact that the dog might have a *home*. She had just automatically assumed that he was a stray. "But, he's so thin," she said. "I don't think he belongs to anyone."

And if he *did* have owners, they should have taken much better care of him, and not let him get lost.

Her father came in, with a whole bunch of

printed-out information he had found online, as well as the address of the nearest twenty-four-hour veterinary clinic, which was more than fifty miles away.

"Did you call the Animal Medical Center?" her mother asked.

The Animal Medical Center was a famous animal hospital in New York City—and she and her mother both knew that her father was pretty convinced that New York was always the best place to get correct answers.

"Well—yes," her father admitted. "They said I should bring him to a vet right away."

Her mother checked the clock on the wall again. "If we leave now, it's going to take us about an hour to get there. So I think we should wait for Dr. K. to—"

Just then, the telephone rang.

When her father answered, Emily could tell right away that their vet, Dr. K., was on the other end. Her father answered quick questions, listened to a few instructions, and then bent down to look at the dog's mouth.

"Yes," he said into the receiver. "I'm afraid his gums *are* quite pale." He listened for another minute, and then held the telephone near the dog's head—probably so that their vet could hear the way he was breathing. Then, her father lifted the telephone back up to his ear, and listened again. "Yes, right away. Thank you." He hung up the phone. "Okay, he's going to meet us over there, with a couple of his technicians."

It took about ten minutes to get the dog safely out to the car. Actually, they had two cars—her mother's Prius, and her father's old Subaru wagon, but her parents had already decided that it would be easier to try and transport the dog in the Subaru, since it was bigger.

Her father lifted one end of the sled, while Emily and her mother carried the other side. They had to walk very slowly, both because the dog was heavy, and because they didn't want to jar him at all. Once they had made it out to the driveway, Emily went ahead to open the door so that her parents could ease the sled onto the backseat.

Her parents agreed to let her sit in the back, to keep the dog company. They were probably still a little worried that she might get bitten, but by now, the dog seemed to be half-conscious and wouldn't be able to bite her, even if he wanted to—which Emily knew he didn't.

Once she had snapped on her seat belt, she put

her hand very lightly on top of the blanket, near the dog's shoulder. He moved his head just enough to rest it on her leg, and she patted him during the entire ride.

When they pulled into the parking lot of Oceanside Animal Hospital, Dr. K. was waiting outside, wearing a white lab coat over a polo shirt and jeans. He was a very tall man, with a beard and glasses, who looked sort of like the medical version of a lumberjack. Two of his assistants were there, too, holding a stretcher. As soon as they saw the car, they all hurried over.

Emily got out, so that Dr. K. could lean into the backseat and perform a very fast examination. He used his stethoscope to check the dog's heart and lungs, and frowned slightly. Then, he lifted the blankets to look the dog over, felt his rib cage and legs, and frowned again.

"Let's get him inside right away," he said to the two technicians. "The pneumothorax is critical."

Working together, Dr. K. and his assistants eased the dog and his blankets out of the car and directly onto the stretcher. Then, they rushed into the office, while Emily's father held the door for them.

There was no time to lose!

"We're going to take him into the back and have

a closer look, okay?" Dr. K. said, sounding very urgent. "I'll come out here and talk to you as soon as I know anything."

Emily was pretty sure that almost twelve was too old to cry in public, but she definitely *felt* like it. "Shouldn't we be in there with him? So he won't be scared?"

Dr. K. shook his head. "No, I'm sorry. It'll be easier right now if you wait out here. But I promise that we're going to do everything we can for him."

With that, he and the techs and the dog disappeared through the swinging doors into the surgical area.

Emily and her parents stood in the middle of the empty room.

"Well, we're in the right place," Emily's mother said. "And he's an *excellent* vet, so we know the dog's in good hands."

Emily nodded, and they sat down in a row of chairs to wait. When her father leaned his head back against the wall and closed his eyes, Emily remembered that *none* of them had gotten much sleep. It wasn't even eight in the morning yet—but she felt as though she had been awake for about a week and a half.

Almost the only times she had ever been to the

vet's office were for Josephine's regular check-ups, the time they had brought her in to be spayed, and once a few months earlier, when she had gotten an upper respiratory infection. After Emily had made up her mind that she wanted to be a veterinarian herself someday, Dr. K. had invited her to spend a couple of afternoons watching the vets and their assistants do routine exams and procedures. It had been very interesting, and she had always hoped that, when she was old enough, she would be able to get some kind of part-time job in the office, working with all of the animals.

But this time was different. Now, they were here with an injured dog who she *already* loved—and he might be too badly hurt to survive.

They sat in the waiting room for what seemed like a *long* time. A *really* long time. Since the office wasn't officially open yet, it was very quiet. The overhead lights were off, which made Emily feel very sleepy, but she *forced* herself to stay awake. Her mother held her hand, which normally might have made her feel a little babyish, but under the circumstances, she didn't mind at all.

Right before nine o'clock, the office manager and one of the receptionists arrived, and were surprised to find people already there. As they turned on the office computers and began to set up for the day's appointments, an elderly woman showed up with a black-and-white cat who needed his yearly shots, and a stocky red-haired man with a booming voice came in with a small rust-colored poodle.

The other clients seemed to be nice, but it was hard to wait for what might be bad news in front of strangers. Emily sat very straight in her chair the whole time, shaking her head when her mother offered her a magazine, and shaking it again when her father suggested going out to get some doughnuts and milk—or anything else that she might like for breakfast.

Finally, Dr. Kasanofsky came out through the swinging doors. He had changed into green surgical scrubs and looked very solemn. Normally, he always had a big smile on his face, so it was alarming to see his expression so serious. He nodded hello to the woman with the cat and the man with the poodle, and then turned to Emily and her parents.

"Why don't we go step into another room to talk for a minute?" he suggested.

Just hearing that was enough to make Emily's stomach sink. But she pushed herself to her feet, as her parents stood up, too.

"Would you like to be in there with us, or would you rather have me talk to your parents alone, first?" Dr. Kasanofsky asked.

"In there, please," Emily said, without hesitating.

Dr. Kasanofsky glanced at her parents, who nodded reluctantly.

He motioned for them to follow him into an exam room. Emily swallowed, knowing that he must

have bad news, if he wanted to speak to them privately. But she took a deep breath and followed her
parents into the small room. It was maybe dumb,
but she had expected that the dog would be in there
on the examination table, waiting for them—only,
he wasn't.

Once they were inside, Dr. Kasanofsky quietly
closed the door.

"Well," he said, and Emily could see that he
looked tired—or maybe just *sad*. "We're doing
everything we can, but I'm afraid he is not in very
good shape. He has several broken ribs, and one of
them punctured his lung, although we were able to
get it re-inflated. His left foreleg has a compound
fracture, and one of his hips was displaced, too.
We're giving him lots of fluids, to try and make up
for the blood loss and the dehydration, but I'm very
concerned about his kidney function. We have him
stabilized, for now, but there's still some internal
bleeding, and I'm going to have to do more surgery
to locate the source. But, if the damage is as exten-
sive as I suspect it might be, I'm not sure that would
be anything more than a temporary fix."

Emily wasn't completely sure what all of that
meant—other than the fact that it sounded really

bad. "He's, um, he's really thin," she said, mostly because she couldn't think of anything else to say.

Dr. Kasanofsky nodded. "I think he must have been out there on his own for quite some time, because he's very weak and malnourished. That would make it much harder for him to fight off any infections, and I also may be hearing the beginning of some pneumonia setting in. He's, well—it's really not a good prognosis." He sighed. "I'm sorry that I don't have better news."

It was very, very quiet in the room for a minute, and Emily had to blink hard, over and over, to keep from crying.

"Do you think we should—" Emily's father stopped in mid-sentence. "I mean, it sounds as though we may have a very difficult decision to make."

Dr. Kasanofsky let out his breath, and looked sadder than ever. "Yes," he said unhappily. "I'm afraid you do."

Emily stared at her father accusingly when she realized that he was talking about putting the dog to *sleep*. "We can't do that, Dad!" she said. "It would be—we have to *save* him. Why do you just want to give up?"

"It's not giving up," her father said. "But, he's terribly sick, and it doesn't sound as though we should put him through any more of this."

To her, that sounded a whole lot like giving up. Besides, he wasn't sick, he was *injured*, which was different. And he could get well. She was sure he could get better, if they would just give him time to do it.

Her mother put her arm around her. "I know it's very hard, Emily, but we have to think about what's best for him, no matter how sad it will make *us*."

Why did her parents always have to be so *reasonable*? Emily wanted to yell at her—at *all* of them—but she just ducked underneath her mother's arm and focused down at the floor, instead. She shouldn't have come into the room with them, if they weren't even going to let her be part of the decision. Her parents always *said* that they wanted to hear her opinion, but sometimes it seemed like they only meant it if she agreed with them.

Her father came over to try and give her a hug, and she shook her head, stepping out of the way. At this particular moment, she didn't *want* either of them to be nice to her. In fact, she pretty much just wanted to be left alone.

There was a folding chair in the corner, near

the small refrigerator where the vets stored medication—and sometimes sodas—and she went over and sat down in it. The chair was angled so that she was facing away from all of them—which was totally fine with her.

Nobody said anything for a moment.

Her mother was the first one to break the silence. "Dr. K., is treating him any further the right thing to do?"

Dr. Kasanofsky sighed. "To be honest, I'm not sure. I'd like to give him every possible chance, but it may not be—" He sighed again. "This is a very difficult situation. His injuries are so severe that I'm not sure he can recover, and there's a good chance that he'll be permanently impaired if he does. And that's if we get lucky, and there are no other complications. At best, he would have a very long recuperation, and he might not ever be able to walk comfortably."

All of that was probably true, but then, why had the dog seemed *so alive*? So happy to be rescued? "But, he worked so hard," Emily said quietly, still sitting in the folding chair. "All by himself. You know, to make sure that someone would find him. That means he wants us to try and save him."

Dr. Kasanofsky nodded. "Yes, I think you're

probably right, Emily. That's what makes these decisions so complicated—*we just don't know* a lot of the time."

That was a good answer, because it made her feel as though her opinion was going to be taken seriously. She *didn't* want the dog to be in pain, or to do anything that would make it harder for him—but, just letting him go felt all wrong. So she turned around in her chair to look at Dr. Kasanofsky directly.

"What would you do if he was your dog?" she asked.

"I really don't know." Dr. Kasanofsky folded his arms and leaned back against the wall to think about that. "His prognosis is very poor—but he's also clearly quite young. And the fact that he's survived this long tells me that he's unusually strong and determined." He paused. "It's not a decision I can make for the three of you, but I can tell you that he's as comfortable as we can make him right now. So I think we could just watch him very closely for the rest of the day, and see how he responds. Then, we can talk again."

Emily was definitely in favor of that, and fortunately, her parents agreed, too.

So they went back to the waiting room and sat,

and sat, and sat some more. Other clients came in and out for appointments, and it was noisy, as cats complained inside their carriers and dogs barked at each other.

After a while, her father left to go pick up some lunch for all of them. Emily was beginning to feel really claustrophobic in the waiting room, so she decided to go outside for a while and get some fresh air. She never would have guessed that sitting and doing nothing could be so completely tiring.

Like most places in Bailey's Cove, the animal hospital was right by the ocean and had its own little dock. Sometimes—especially when the snow was so deep that it was difficult to drive—Dr. K. and his assistants would pay house calls, by *boat*.

It was still raining, and so chilly that it felt more like late fall than summer. She had left her slicker in the waiting room, but getting wet seemed more appealing than going back inside.

Emily walked across the parking lot, and then down the neat gravel path to the dock. Her knee was still kind of stiff, but it didn't hurt that much, and she only limped a little. There were a bunch of big rock formations along the side of the path, and she decided to climb up on top of one of them. The granite was so wet that her sneakers slipped a little, but she was able to pull herself up without too much trouble.

Then, she sat there, staring out at the ocean. This part of town was in a protected cove, so even during storms, the water was usually pretty calm. Today, it looked dark grey, and tiny waves slapped gently against the dock every so often. Because of the weather, there didn't seem to be any pleasure boats out, which was really unusual in August. A few stray seagulls swooped around, looking for food, and she saw a loon, too. Other than that, it looked like a quiet autumn day.

Sitting alone on the rock was private, and so she let herself cry a little. She knew Dr. K. and his assistants were trying to do everything they could to save the dog, but it didn't sound as though it was going to work.

Neither of her parents was really into the idea of pets, especially her father, but they had always had at least one cat, because Emily had been crazy about animals as far back as she could remember. She loved Josephine, who they had had for about five years, and couldn't imagine life without her. But she had *always* wanted a dog, too. It was almost exactly a month until her birthday, and after she had nagged them pretty much nonstop for the past year or two, her parents had promised her that they would talk seriously about going over to the animal shelter and picking one out.

But, she wanted *this* dog. It was maybe stupid to feel so attached to an animal she had only known for a couple of hours, but she did. She felt—connected. Every time he had looked at her with those sad, deep brown eyes, it had seemed as though he somehow knew everything that she was thinking and feeling.

She couldn't stand the thought of losing this dog—but, right now, there wasn't anything she could do to help him.

All she could do was hope.

Emily stayed on the rock, in the rain, for a long time, lost in thought.

"I thought you might want this," a voice said.

Emily looked up to see that her mother had come outside and was holding her yellow slicker. "No, thanks," she said. "I'm okay."

Normally, her mother would have told her to put it on, anyway, but she just nodded and set the coat down on one of the other rocks.

"Your father just called, and he'll be back in a few minutes," she said. "You didn't have any breakfast, so I want you to try and eat a decent lunch, okay?"

She wasn't at all hungry, but Emily nodded.

Her mother nodded, too, and climbed up effortlessly to sit next to her on the rock. The rain was still coming down pretty hard, and they both watched as a small lobster boat chugged across the water, stopping every so often at a brightly-marked buoy so that the man and the woman in the boat could check their traps and set out a few new ones.

"Do you think he hurts?" Emily asked, after a while.

Her mother shook her head. "No. They're giving him medicine to help him sleep, and to make sure he isn't in any pain."

Did animals take things like aspirin or Tylenol? Or did they have special medications? Since he'd been having surgery, though, he might not even be awake yet. For a second, it occurred to her that he might never wake up *at all*, but she wasn't going to let herself think about that.

"No matter what happens," her mother said, "you did the right thing by trying to save him. I'm very proud of you."

That was a nice compliment, and Emily nodded, a little bit shyly. "All I did was go outside."

"Well," her mother lifted an eyebrow, "according to your father, you did considerably *more* than that."

Emily checked her expression to see how much trouble she might be in, before answering. "I didn't plan it. It just, you know, *happened*."

Her mother nodded.

"Dad was really mad at me," Emily said.

"No, your father was afraid you might get hurt," her mother corrected her. "There's a big difference."

"I *had* to jump in," Emily said defensively. "Are you going to yell at me about it, too?"

Actually, her parents almost never yelled—at anyone, or about anything. Mostly, they liked to be very calm and reasonable, and *discuss* things. At length. Sometimes, they had really, really *long* discussions—like, for several hours—and once, during a lengthy debate that had sounded a whole lot more like an actual *argument*, her father had even put a kitchen timer on the table to force her mother to wind down a little more efficiently.

"Not today," her mother said, but then she looked at her sharply. "I know you're an excellent swimmer, but that water can be very dangerous, especially during a thunderstorm."

The currents were often so strong, and the part of the sound in front of their house was so deep, that when she wanted to go swimming, her parents drove down to the beach or took her over to the pools at the college. And if she was ever on a boat of any kind, she *always* wore a life jacket.

"So, from now on, I need for you to remember to be much more careful," her mother said.

Emily nodded. Her parents worried *a lot* about

her, and she didn't know if all parents were like that, or whether hers were particularly anxious. She kind of thought that because her parents had been a little bit older when they adopted her, they spent more time worrying than her friends' parents did. Being an only child probably had a lot to do with it, too.

Out in the water, the people in the lobster boat had hauled up another trap. Emily and her mother watched as the man and woman tossed back the lobsters that were too small, collected the ones that were of legal size, and then re-baited the trap and dropped it back into the sea.

"Is it selfish to want them to keep trying?" Emily asked.

Her mother paused to think about that. Unlike her father, who always had *definite* opinions and rarely changed his mind, her mother's fields were political science and constitutional law, and so she was inclined to see both sides of *everything*. "No, not at this point," she said finally. "But, even though I know it's awful, we're going to have to prepare ourselves for what we might have to do."

Emily nodded, feeling an immediate lump in her throat. She had only been about six when their seventeen-year-old cat, Wilbur, had had to be put to sleep, and all she remembered was that her parents came home with an empty carrier, and that her mother had gone into her room and cried straight through dinner. It had been really sad, and after a while, Emily had gone in there and cried, too, both of them cuddled under a thick quilt.

They sat there, in the rain.

"He should have a name," Emily said quietly.

Her mother glanced over.

"If something bad happens, he should have a name and know that people loved him." Just saying the words brought tears to her eyes, and Emily wiped them on her already very wet sleeve.

"Okay," her mother said, and put her arm around her. "What's his name?"

Emily didn't even have to think. "Zack." The name just felt right.

Her mother looked a little surprised by how quickly she had come up with it. "Just Zack?"

"Zachary," Emily said. "But Zack for a nick-name."

"All right, then," her mother said, and tight-ened her arm around her shoulders. "Zack it is."

When they saw her father pulling into the parking lot, Emily jumped down off the rock, landing upright in a puddle with a small splash.

Her father had brought back enough sandwiches, chips, and drinks for everyone who worked in the vet's office, too. Emily still wasn't at all hungry, but to keep her mother from looking so worried, she ate an egg salad sandwich and a little bag of potato chips, and had some orange juice, too.

Then, once all of the food and drinks were gone, it was back to waiting. The only news they had gotten at all was when Gary, one of the techs, came out and told them that the dog—Zack!—was back in surgery. Other than that, they just waited.

None of them talked much, but she was glad that her parents were both there to keep her company. Every minute seemed to last an hour, and every hour seemed to last a *century*. The office officially closed for the day at six o'clock, but they were allowed to stay and keep waiting.

It was just after seven when Dr. Kasanofsky came out of the back room. Even though he hadn't said anything yet, he was walking so slowly that Emily knew the answer before he even spoke.

"I'm very sorry," he said. "I think it's time."

10

Emily knew that she had to be brave, but it was hard. If their vet was telling them it was time, it was *time*. So she just nodded, and rubbed her hand across her eyes, and pretended to listen while her parents and Dr. Kasanofsky talked. She didn't really want to know the details; all that mattered was that they were going to have to put her dog to sleep.

"Can we see him?" she asked.

"Of course," Dr. Kasanofsky said. "Let me just go in the back for a minute, and then the three of you can join me."

While they were waiting, Emily cried a little, and her parents hugged her. They both looked close to tears, too.

Linda, the other vet technician, came out and gestured for them to follow her into a small examining room in the back. The lights had been turned low, and the dog was lying on his side on top of some thick towels, on a metal examining table. His eyes were closed, and he was hooked up to an IV and various other tubes.

The first thing Emily noticed was that, for such a big dog, he looked very *small* now. He was covered with bandages, and stitches, and there were lots of bare patches where his fur had been shaved. His skin was almost pink under the white fur, which surprised her, for some reason. There was also a large cast on his left front leg.

Looking at him, Emily understood why the hard decision was the right one. The dog was frail and weak, and barely seemed to be breathing at all.

Dr. Kasanofsky put his hand on her shoulder. "I'm very sorry. He was just too badly hurt."

Emily nodded. She wouldn't have said that she was crying, but she could feel tears running down her cheeks. "Is he in pain?" she asked.

Dr. Kasanofsky shook his head. "No. I don't think he can really feel anything at all now. He's just very, very tired."

Someone—she wasn't sure who—handed her some Kleenex, and she wiped her eyes. "C-can I say good-bye?"

"Of course," Dr. Kasanofsky said. "Why don't the three of you spend some time with him? Take as long as you need."

With that, he and the two vet technicians left the room, closing the door behind them.

Once they were by themselves, all three of them cried, and her parents took turns hugging her.

"I'm really sorry," her father said. "I wish there was something I could say to help."

Her mother gave her some more Kleenex, which Emily gratefully accepted. "I know," she said. "I just—I was sure he was going to be okay." She had *felt* it.

There really wasn't anything else to say, so they all just stood there next to the examining table.

"Could I be alone with him?" Emily asked. "Just, you know, for a minute?"

Her parents exchanged glances, and then nodded.

"We'll be right outside if you need us," her mother said.

Once they were gone, Emily looked miserably at the dog. He hadn't moved once, in the entire time they had been in here. As awful as it was to admit, he looked as though he was *already* gone. She had never really thought about life, and death, in a serious way, and what it all meant. Staring at the dog—at *Zack*—she wondered if he knew she was there, or if he was too far away from them now.

"I named you," she said softly. "That'll seem dumb, but I thought you needed a name. I mean, I know you can't hear me, but I wanted you to know that you *belonged* to someone." Now she was crying again, and it was hard to speak. "That you weren't by yourself. And that you were *brave*."

She didn't know if she was allowed to touch him, but if she was careful, she was pretty sure that she wouldn't make things worse than they already were.

She started to reach her hand out, but then hesitated. Would he feel cold? And stiff? And—well—not alive?

For a minute, she was afraid to find out, but almost as quickly, she was ashamed that she had even thought something like that. Her parents were right—none of this was about her, it was about the dog. About *Zack*.

She walked around to the other side of the table, so that she would be behind him. That way, she could pat his head with her right hand and drape her left arm over his chest and shoulder. It wouldn't *quite* be a hug, but it would be close.

She bent over him, sliding her hand underneath his head, so it would be sort of like a pillow.

"You are such a good boy," she whispered into his ear. "I'm really sorry I never got to do *dog* stuff with you. I could have thrown you sticks, and tennis balls, and given you food under the table when my parents weren't looking, and—well, anything you wanted."

It felt almost as though he had moved a little, responding to her voice, but she knew that was just wishful thinking.

"I would have taken *really* good care of you, Zack," she said. "We would have gotten you your own red bowl—" Unless, maybe, he didn't *like* red? "Or maybe a blue bowl. A blue bowl would have been good. Not one of those, you know, stainless steel ones."

She waited, to see if he might move, but he just lay there with his eyes closed.

"We would have gone for lots of walks," she said. "All around town. And you'd get to ride in the car, and stick your nose out the window, and all of that good stuff. I would have been the best owner I could." No, that didn't sound right. "I mean, I would have been the best *friend* I could be."

She wondered, then, whether she had been in here too long, and if her parents and Dr. Kasanofsky were going to come in soon?

"You're *so* good," she whispered, and then hugged him as well as she could, being careful not to dislodge any of the tubes or bandages. "I'll always, *always* remember you."

Okay. Now it really was time.

She gave him a small kiss on the head, and then straightened up. It would be too hard to look at him again, so she kept her head down as she went over to the door.

As she started to turn the doorknob, she thought she heard a sigh behind her. It sounded like that, anyway. But, when she peeked back for a second, he was still lying in the same position, so it must have been her imagination.

Then, she heard the sound again.

Only this time, it was—clearly, distinctly, *unmistakably*—a very small *woof.*

11

Emily spun around and stared at the examining table.

"Zack?" she said, uncertainly.

It was hard to tell in the dim light, but she was almost sure that his eyes were open.

"Zack? Are you okay?" she asked.

He lifted his head, and then moved—laboriously—until he was sitting up partway.

Whoa. "Mom!" she yelled. "Dad! Come quick!"

The door flew open, and within less than a minute, her parents and Dr. Kasanofsky had all raced in.

"Look, he's okay!" she said.

They looked at the table, and exchanged glances.

Emily couldn't figure out why they weren't more excited, until she saw that the dog was back on his side, with his eyes closed.

"No, you don't understand, he moved," she said. "He sat up."

Dr. Kasanofsky looked awkward. "It might have

82

seemed like that, Emily, but it was probably just an involuntary muscle—"

"No, he *sat up*," Emily said.

They all stared at her the way the characters had stared at Dorothy in the last scene of *The Wizard of Oz*.

"He really did," she said defensively. "And he barked, too."

None of them patted her on the head, or said, "Of course he did, dear," but she was afraid that they might.

Instead of shouting "Please, wake up!" at the dog—which she sort of did, inside her head, she rested her hand on his side. "Zack," she said, very quietly.

After a long second, the dog opened his eyes. He held her gaze, and then made that sighing sound, and painfully began to climb to his feet. It seemed to take forever, and Emily held her breath the whole time. Since his left foreleg wouldn't support any weight, he stood on the other three legs, so shaky that she was afraid he would topple over.

He steadied himself, the cast hanging awkwardly in the air, and then wagged his tail a couple of times.

The room was absolutely silent. "*Wow*," Gary, one of the vet techs, said from the doorway.

"Wow" was an understatement!

After that, everything seemed to move very fast. Dr. Kasanofsky examined Zack, and his vital signs were strong and steady. He would still have to stay in the hospital for a while, and there were no guarantees, but his prognosis was dramatically better than it had been just an hour earlier.

Dr. Kasanofsky was going to stay late at the office to monitor Zack, and the other vet tech, Linda, would be spending the night, so that he could have twenty-four-hour intensive care. Emily was nervous about leaving him, but she knew that he would be in very good hands.

It wasn't until they got home, and were sitting at the dinner table, that Emily realized how exhausted she was. Her parents were kind of dozing over their plates, too, which made sense, because the three of them had had barely any sleep.

"Long day," her father said finally.

Boy, *that* was for sure.

After supper, they all sat in the den to watch the Red Sox for a while, but Emily just couldn't stay awake.

"Maybe a shower, and some sleep?" her mother suggested.

Emily nodded. Despite all of the time she had spent sitting in the rain, she still felt muddy and could smell the brine on herself from her dive into the ocean. Sometimes, for her own pride, she liked to pretend that she didn't want to be tucked in and fussed over anymore—but she was always relieved when at least one of her parents still did it, anyway.

"We'll go over to visit him first thing tomorrow morning," her mother said, as she put a fresh satin pillowcase on Emily's pillow. Her mother always worried that cotton pillowcases might be too harsh on her hair, and made sure that she deep-conditioned and moisturized her hair regularly, and didn't shampoo too much. Her mother also, unsurprisingly, had a large collection of books about how to take care of and style African-American hair— and followed the instructions *religiously*. In the meantime, her father would say things like, "Can't she just *brush* it, and leave it at that?"

"He'll be okay tonight, right?" Emily asked.

Her mother nodded. "He seems to be a very determined dog."

He seemed to be an *unusually* determined dog.

For once, Emily didn't have any nightmares at

all, and she woke up feeling pretty energetic, although her nose was a little stuffed up. That was probably just hay fever or something, though.

After she got dressed and fed Josephine, she checked her email and found a stack of about eight new messages from friends who were surprised she hadn't been online at all the night before—which was, of course, *totally* unusual—and one from her cousin Ronald, too. She answered each of them with a version of "I found a dog! Will let you know more later" and then closed her laptop.

When she went downstairs, her parents were already sitting at the kitchen table, eating breakfast and plowing through a stack of newspapers. Her father was looking sloppy—and sleepy—in pajama pants and an old striped Oxford shirt, while her mother must have already been out kayaking, because her hair was wet and she was still wearing aqua shoes and a water-repellant splash shirt over her shorts.

"Sleep well?" her father asked, drinking some coffee.

Emily nodded. "Yeah. Thanks. There weren't, um, any bad messages from the vet's, right?"

Her mother shook her head. "No, and I went out to get every local paper I could find this morning, to see if anyone reported him missing. We haven't come across anything so far."

Good. Yay, even!

"I have some work I need to get done this morning," her father said, "but you and your mother can go over to Oceanside and see how he is in the meantime. Just in case someone really did lose him, Dr. Kasanofsky is putting the word out to the other vets, and all of the animal shelters, too."

Emily nodded, knowing that she should be smart and stay *cautiously* optimistic, but she was starting to feel *genuinely* optimistic. After having eaten almost no dinner the night before, she was really hungry and easily finished several pieces of French toast, along with some cut-up strawberries and a glass of chocolate milk. She had never liked the taste of plain milk, but her parents had agreed that it was worth the trade-off of having her drink more milk, as long as it had a little bit of flavoring—okay, *sugar*—in it.

When she went outside, she saw her friend Bobby pedaling down the street past her house on his bike. To be specific, he was riding no-hands, with his arms folded across his chest—because, lately, he had decided that he was mostly too cool to ride the normal way. He saw her and put on the brakes, lowering his hands onto the handlebars to keep his balance.

She walked over to meet him. "Hi, Bobby."

"*Bob*," he said.

Emily grinned. At his twelfth birthday party back in June, he had insisted that he now wanted to be known only as "Bob." Or, he had said, "Sir" would be okay, too. She told him she would call him that, if he referred to *her* as "Your Highness" or "Your Lordship." But, since Emily had met him when they were barely three years old, she still automatically called him "Bobby" without thinking. He was the only other kid her age in the neighborhood, so it was a good thing that they had always gotten along really well. In a lot of ways, they didn't have much in common—he loved fishing and playing lacrosse, and *didn't* like school, but he was always funny and cheerful, and they had a great time goofing around together. They would ride their bikes, or climb around on the rocks in front of one of their houses, or spend hours shooting baskets with his older brother and sister.

And the birthday party had been really *fun*, because his parents had taken fifteen of them to the water park near Old Orchard Beach. She had liked it so much that she was thinking of asking her parents if they could do the same thing for her birthday, in September.

"Hello, Robert," she said.

He laughed. "Yup. Okay." Then, he leaned down with his elbows resting against the handlebars, which made him much closer to her height. Bobby had grown a lot in the last year or so—and that included his hair, which was long, thick, and sandy blond. Her friend Karen always said that he looked like a big old hippie. "I am *so* too cool to ride by your house and stuff, but it seemed like, you know, no one was home at all yesterday."

Emily nodded. "I know, we weren't." Her throat was hurting a little, and she coughed a couple of times. Sometimes, she got allergies, so maybe there was a bunch of pollen in the air today? "I rescued a dog, and we didn't get home until pretty late."

"Cool. Can I see him?" Bobby asked.

"I found him over on the rocks, and he was bleeding and everything," Emily said, gesturing towards the Peabodys' house. "So he's still at the vet's, but they're pretty sure he's going to be okay."

"What kind is he?" Bobby asked.

He was probably a mongrel, but there was something so elegant and distinctive about him that she wondered if he might be some rare, valuable breed she just didn't know about. "He looks like a retriever, sort of, except he's all white," Emily said. "I named him Zack. Well, I mean, Zachary, but *Zack*, mostly."

Bobby motioned towards the house, where her mother was on her way out to the driveway. "They going to let you keep him?"

On the whole, they probably didn't have much of a *choice*—and besides, she assumed her parents were already pretty fond of him, too. Emily nodded. "Yeah. Even though Dad thinks he's kind of too big. I don't think he belongs to anyone, because he's all thin and everything." She looked at him uneasily. "Have you heard of anyone who lost a dog?"

Bobby thought for a second, then shook his head. "Nope. But Mr. Johnson's horse got out again and was running all over yesterday. Andrea"—who was his big sister—"said he was in Mrs. Griswold's yard, and she was going wicked crazy about it and screaming and stuff."

Mrs. Griswold was this mean older lady who lived by herself about six houses down, and never seemed to come outside, except when she was yelling at people. She didn't have a car, so she always rode an old black bicycle around to do her errands, and some people called her Miss Gulch—from the character in *The Wizard of Oz*—behind her back. Whenever Emily went past her house on her way to visit Bobby and his family, or go watch the boats at the wharf, she stayed on the other side of the road—and walked quickly. Her parents—who were invariably very, very polite—always just said that Mrs. Griswold was "eccentric." Emily probably would have gone with "scary."

"Good morning, Bobby," Emily's mother said, as she opened the car door. "Please thank your father for the lobsters. If they ever start *growing*, I'll bring some of my vegetables over for all of you."

Her mother could do a lot of things really well—but, even though she worked hard on it and read lots of instruction books, so far, gardening did not seem to be one of them.

Bobby grinned, but then nodded enthusiastically. Probably *too* enthusiastic to be convincing. "Thank you, Mrs. Feingold."

"You may not want to hold your breath, though, until it happens," Emily's mother said wryly.

"It's a *nice* garden," Emily said. "The weeds are very pretty." And there were *a lot* of them. Although, personally, she liked the way the dandelions looked. A lot of people in Maine were crazy about dandelion greens, and sometimes, one of their neighbors would come over and ask to dig a few up for a salad or stew the person was making.

Her mother sighed. "I know. They are getting a little out of control, aren't they? Well, maybe this weekend, we can spend some time pulling—"

Just then, the back door flew open, and Emily's father hurried outside.

"I'm sorry, they just called from the animal hospital," he said urgently. "We need to get over there right away!"

12

On the ride over, Emily was so tense that it was hard to breathe. Her chest felt tight, and her throat hurt, too. Oceanside had not told her father many details, other than the fact that Zack had taken a sudden turn for the worse, and was now back in intensive care.

When they arrived at the vet's, it turned out that Zack had developed pneumonia and was being given oxygen and strong antibiotics. He was also going to get regular treatments in something called a nebulizer, which was like a huge vaporizer and was supposed to help his lungs work more easily. He was actually in the middle of a treatment at that very moment, and they were going to have to stay in the waiting room until it was finished.

A really weird thing was that she must be having sympathy pains or something, because she had been coughing on and off in the car, and felt like she might even be running a fever.

"Are you all right?" her mother asked anxiously. "You don't look very good, Emily."

Except for a little bit of a stuffed nose, she had felt perfectly fine when she woke up, so this must be like, hypochondria or something. Or—was that the right word? "I think I'm just worried about Zack," Emily said.

But, her chest *did* hurt, and that was creepy. She caught herself rubbing her sternum without thinking, and immediately stopped, because she didn't want her parents to notice.

However, her mother must have seen her, because she reached over and felt her forehead. "You're a little warm, Em," she said, and frowned. "Maybe you're coming down with something."

"It might be, like, ragweed," Emily said uncertainly. "I was coughing a couple of times when I was talking to Bobby."

Plus, of course, she was *upset* now, and that was bound to make her feel pretty bad.

The waiting room was crowded—with people, dogs, cats, and even a guinea pig, so her father was pacing around, and stepped outside every so often so that he wouldn't be surrounded by so many animals. There was only one free chair, and her mother wanted her to take it, but Emily would have felt guilty about that, so they shared it. Her mother was pretty small, so they had had a habit of sitting together that way for years, anyway.

But, right now, it was too close for comfort, because her mother was watching her so closely.

"Maybe I have, you know, hypochondria," Emily said, whispering so that no one else would hear them. "Because I'm so worried about him."

Her mother's arm, which was around her, relaxed slightly. "That's true," she agreed. "Although I wouldn't call that hypochondria, I'd call that empathy. Take a few deep breaths, and see if it helps."

It hurt to take deep breaths, but since she knew it was just in her head, Emily did it, anyway.

"He's a very strong dog," her mother said. "We'll just have to pray that this is a temporary setback."

Emily nodded, taking another deep breath. The floor in the clinic must have been mopped recently or something, because there was a very strong medicine smell all around them. An overpowering smell that was making her a little dizzy. She wanted to ask her mother if she could smell it, too—but she had already been weird enough for one morning.

"Was hypochondria the right word?" she asked, to distract herself. "I feel like there's another one."

Her parents *loved* words, so any conversation about language was guaranteed to be lively—and *lengthy*.

Her mother nodded. "You're probably thinking of 'psychosomatic.' It's similar, but not quite the same—" She broke off her sentence, as they both saw Dr. Kasanofsky come out of the back and motion towards them. Emily quickly went to the outside door, and when her father—who had been in the parking lot—saw her, he hurried back into the building.

Once she and her parents went into the same private examining room where they had been the day before, Dr. Kasanofsky looked so solemn that Emily knew that Zack's condition had to be grave.

"I'm very sorry," he said to them. "I know we discussed the possibility of pneumonia yesterday, but I was hoping that the antibiotics would kick in before that happened. He has lots of fight in him, but he's so weak that he may not be able to rally past this, on top of everything else."

Emily swallowed, her throat hurting worse than ever. "Do we have to put him to sleep?"

Dr. Kasanofsky hesitated, but then nodded reluctantly. "Right now, we're looking at intubation as our next step and, to be honest, that may be further than we want to go. If his breathing continues to be this severely impaired, I'm afraid that would be my recommendation, yes."

Oh. She hadn't been expecting such a definite answer, and she had to rub her hand across her eyes as they filled with tears.

Her mother came over to hug her, which made her feel a little better, but not that much.

"May we see him?" Emily's mother asked.

Dr. Kasanofsky nodded. "Yes, I think it might be very helpful, so they're setting it up right now. He's just come out of the nebulizer. We've been monitoring his blood gases very carefully, too, so that we can decide what steps we want to take with his oxygen treatment. Let me go see how they're doing."

They had to wait for a few more minutes, and then Gary, one of the techs, came to get them.

Zack was in what looked like an intensive care cage, well padded with towels. His breathing was very labored, and he was coughing feebly, too. He seemed to have even more tubes and IVs than he had the day before, and there was some thick, folded plastic next to him.

"That's the oxygen hood," Dr. Kasanofsky explained. "Unfortunately, it has been causing him some anxiety, so we may have to sedate him to be able to use it. Right now"—he pointed at a thin, plastic tube—"we're trying to direct a small flow towards him and see if that helps."

Emily could smell the intense medicine scent more strongly than ever, and wondered if it was from his medication, and not floor cleaner, after all. Her chest felt as though someone was squeezing her lungs tightly together, and out of nowhere, she felt a wave of fear so intense that she couldn't focus on anything else.

She realized that someone was talking to her, and shook her head to try and snap out of it.

"It's okay if you want to pat him," Dr. Kasanofsky said.

Emily nodded, and reached forward tentatively.

Her dog was trembling, and it seemed as though the fear was coming directly *from* him.

"It's okay," she said, and stroked him soothingly on the head. "You're going to be okay. They're giving you medicine, to help you feel better."

She could feel the trembling ease, and—he seemed calmer, somehow. He even seemed to be breathing more easily.

Dr. Kasanofsky moved in next to her with his stethoscope. "No, please keep patting him," he said, when she started to step aside.

So Emily did, while Dr. Kasanofsky listened intently to whatever it was he was hearing through the stethoscope.

"Okay," he said. "Would you please move away for a minute?"

She had no idea why he would want her to do that, but she hesitated and then withdrew.

Dr. Kasanofsky waited a couple of minutes, and then pressed the stethoscope to Zack's chest again. "Interesting," he said, when he was finished, sounding as though he was talking to himself. Then he looked up. "Gary, will you come over and pat him now?"

Gary shrugged and did it.

Once again, Dr. Kasanofsky waited before he checked Zack's vital signs, and then nodded to himself.

Emily glanced at her parents, who were both too busy watching curiously to notice.

Dr. Kasanofsky straightened up, briefly draping the stethoscope over his shoulder. "Emily, will you humor me, and go out to the waiting room for about ten minutes? I'll have one of your parents come get you."

She knew he was a very good veterinarian—and a nice person, to boot, but Emily still looked at him suspiciously. "You're not going to put him to sleep, and just don't want me to see, right?"

Dr. Kasanofsky shook his head. "No, I promise. I'm trying an experiment here, that's all."

Emily didn't like it, but she went. Instead of going all the way out to the waiting room, she decided to stay in the corridor, where she leaned against the wall, folding her arms nervously across her chest.

After a couple of minutes, her father joined her.

"Did he kick you out, too?" Emily asked.

"Just keeping you company," her father said.

Emily nodded, and they stood there quietly.

"You don't really like dogs," she said, after a minute.

Her father started to shake his head, and stopped. "Well—I'm not really *used* to them. I've never had one before. But I sure like *Zack*."

She hoped so. Because it *mattered* to her that he liked him, especially since he wasn't really an animal person.

It seemed to take forever, but finally, her mother appeared in the doorway and waved them back inside.

As soon as she touched him, Emily could feel that Zack had gotten very scared again, while she was gone. Dr. Kasanofsky had her go through the whole patting/stethoscope ritual one more time, and then nodded to himself, looking very pleased.

"Zack has *really* bonded to you, Emily," he said, as he stuck the stethoscope into the pocket of his lab coat. "When he's by himself, his vital signs are terrible, but they improve slightly when one of us rests a hand on him. But, when *you* pat him, his respiration and heart rate are almost completely normal."

Emily was puzzled. Why would it be surprising that her dog would feel better when she was there?

"It's *dramatic*, Emily," Dr. Kasanofsky said. "He moves from being critical to stable in just a minute or two. Then, when you're not here, he swings right down again. It's—well, there's no good medical explanation for it, frankly."

She still wasn't really following him.

"Let me put it this way," he said. "The more time you spend with him, the more likely it is that he just might pull through."

Oh.

Wow!

13

Emily's parents wouldn't actually let her spend the *night* at the veterinary hospital—and Dr. Kasanofsky probably wouldn't have, either—but, as long as she ate and slept properly, and took lots of breaks during the day, they agreed that she could stay there with him during most of the hours that the clinic was open.

Over the next few days, Zack continued to improve steadily. Her parents drove her back and forth constantly, and every single time, her dog would perk up as soon as she walked into the room. Dr. Kasanofsky wanted them to encourage him to eat, so each time, Emily would bring some kind of special treat with her like Milk-Bones, or beef jerky, or some special freeze-dried liver bits that Ms. Sheldon, who ran the pet store, recommended. Zack *really liked* the liver bits.

One of her parents always kept her company, although mostly, they just sat and read quietly or worked. She would mostly pat the dog, and talk to him. It always *felt* like he was listening to every word she said, and she told him all about Josephine, and what their house was like, and how she couldn't wait until it was time for him to come and live with them for good.

Usually, she liked to spend some time every day drawing or painting, so she would bring a sketch pad along with her. Her parents had enrolled her in lots of different after-school and summer art classes, so that she could learn different techniques, but a few simple pencils and erasers were still her favorites. Zack was a good subject—with his alert eyes and his floppy ears—and she drew him from lots of different angles, filling up half a pad of paper in about three days.

Sometimes, especially in the late afternoons, she would doze off, and as often as not, Zack would fall asleep, too. The nebulizer treatments seemed to make him extra tired, but every day, his breathing was getting better, and he had stopped coughing as much. The other good news was that none of the animal shelters or other veterinarians in the southern part of Maine had had *anyone* report a missing white dog!

To help Zack's lungs heal, Dr. Kasanofsky

taught her a technique called coupage. She would bend her hand partway and then move it around his chest with gentle taps, which was supposed to loosen the moisture inside his lungs and help him cough it away. Usually, Dr. Kasanofsky or one of the vet techs did the coupage themselves, but sometimes, they watched her try it for a couple of minutes, too, to make sure that she was doing it right.

Dr. Kasanofsky also wanted him to start exercising a little bit, so twice a day, they would walk very slowly around the room a couple of times. Emily was afraid that it would hurt him too much to put weight on his cast, but Zack seemed comfortable using only three legs—and very happy to be moving around. She felt claustrophobic just sitting *next* to the cage where he was recuperating, so she couldn't imagine how confined it must feel to be *inside* it.

Even though the walks were so short, Zack would wag his tail the entire time. Then, when he started to get tired, he would lean the side of his head against her leg, and she would know that it was time to stop, and would get someone to lift him back up onto an examining table or into the cage.

On Friday afternoon, Dr. Kasanofsky said that it

would be okay for them to try going outside for the first time. So the three of them—along with her mother—took a very slow stroll around the parking lot.

Zack wagged his tail nonstop, moving along with lots of energy, and he even stopped once to bark at a seagull. He also sniffed the air for a long time, and then walked directly over to her parents' car, nosing the passenger-side door curiously.

Emily looked over at Dr. Kasanofsky, who had a broad smile on his face. "What do you think, Dr. K.?" she asked.

"I think I'm going to send him home first thing tomorrow morning," Dr. Kasanofsky said.

Emily was so excited that she bent down to give Zack as big—and careful—a hug as she could. "Do you hear that?" she said. "You're coming home!"

Zack wagged his tail even harder, and barked again.

As far as she could tell, he was as happy about it as she was!

On their way back to the house, she and her mother stopped at the pet store to buy a bunch of supplies. They picked out a red plaid collar with a matching leash, a big fleece bed with a blue cotton cover, canned and dry food, beef and cheese-flavored biscuits, a couple of bones for him to chew, a brush and a comb, a hard rubber ball, and a package of tennis balls.

"How about these?" her mother asked, pointing towards a set of chrome food and water dishes, which looked a lot like the ones in his cage at the vet's.

Emily shook her head. "He doesn't like metal. It hurts his teeth."

Her mother blinked. "Oh. Well, okay. Which ones do you think he would like, then?"

Emily glanced at the different kinds of dishes displayed and knew the right answer immediately. "The blue ones. And they'll match his bed."

Her mother shrugged, and put the plastic bowls into their shopping cart.

"I know it's a lot of stuff, Mom," Emily said. "But, is it okay if we get something for Josephine, too? So her feelings won't be hurt?"

Her mother smiled. "That sounds like a good idea."

So they bought Josephine something called a catnip mat, which Mrs. Sheldon assured them cats *loved* to sleep and play around on, and a new ceramic food dish with tiny flowers on it. Maybe Josephine didn't actually care one way or the other, but Emily had always thought that her cat preferred things that were *pretty*.

She and her mother had called ahead to tell her father the good news, and when they got home, he had already cleared out a large space on the den floor to put Zack's new bed.

"Um, thank you," Emily said, "but isn't he going to sleep in my room?"

"Oh." Her father frowned. "I don't know. Is that what dogs do?"

She and her mother nodded.

"Okay, then," her father said, then shrugged and carried the fleece bed upstairs.

After supper, it occurred to Emily that Zack might not feel strong enough to climb the stairs, or that trying to do it might make his leg hurt. So, while her mother was working on a syllabus for one of the political science classes she was going to be teaching that semester, Emily and her father decided to *make* an extra dog bed, which they would put in the den, just in case.

"And this way, he can be in here with us when we watch movies and stuff," Emily said.

"That's right," her father said, and indicated the television, where the Red Sox were losing by nine runs in the fifth inning. "We certainly wouldn't want him to miss things like *that*."

Emily grinned. "Maybe he'll heal quicker if we don't ever let him see really bad scores."

Her father nodded. "I know it would improve *my* health."

It took a pretty long time, but they carefully cut an oversized cardboard box down until it was the perfect size for a dog bed, and neatly piled old beach towels inside for padding. When they were finished, Emily used different colored Magic Markers to write "Zachary" on the outside, and drew a few bones and balls and birds and things on the cardboard, too.

Josephine ambled downstairs, sniffed at the bed, and then curled up in the middle of it, on top of the towels. Emily had expected that, since she had completely ignored her new catnip mat and gone to sleep on the fleece bed the second her father had put it in her bedroom.

"I think old Zack's going to have some competition," her father said.

Emily nodded. It sure looked that way.

She was just finishing her drawings when her mother came down from her office to see how they were doing. "What do you think, Mom?"

Her mother bent down to examine the bed—and give Josephine a pat while she was at it. "Very nice," she said. "I'd sleep in it myself."

Which Emily thought was really funny to picture.

After the Red Sox lost—by only one run, after *almost* coming back to win in the bottom of the ninth, they went out to the kitchen to have some ice cream. Her father always said that it was very important to seek some small comfort—preferably in the form of sweets—after demoralizing defeats.

She was pretty sure that it would be impossible to get to sleep at all that night, but she must have been more tired than she thought, because she dropped off in the middle of reading a chapter in her latest book.

When she woke up, the book was still lying across her chest, and the sun was shining through her windows. She lifted her book, to pick up where she had left off, and then remembered that this wasn't an ordinary, lazy summer morning.

Today was the day that her dog was coming home!

14

Emily and her parents drove over to the animal hospital so that they would be there right when it opened. In fact, Emily had been so eager for them not to be late that they ended up arriving half an hour early. Rhoda, the office manager, laughed when she saw them waiting in the parking lot.

"Pretty excited?" she asked, as she unlocked the front door of the building to let them in.

"*Very* excited," Emily said.

Once Zack had had one last examination—and passed with flying colors, Emily put on his new collar and leash. In the meantime, her mother wrote down detailed home-care instructions and gathered together the antibiotics and other medications he was going to have to take for the next few weeks, while her father mostly stood around looking as though he thought they were getting in *way* over their heads. Zack would also have to come back for regular check-ups, to make sure that his lungs were staying clear, and that his injuries were healing.

When they came out to the waiting room, Emily hanging tightly to Zack's leash, the people waiting for appointments must have heard the whole story from Rhoda or someone, because they all clapped.

"That is one lucky dog," a woman said.

Emily was pretty sure that *she* was the lucky one, but she just nodded and thanked the woman, who had a little black-and-white fluff ball of a dog perched on her lap—named, as it turned out, Wolverine.

When they were all finally in the car, her father handed a copy of the bill over to her mother, who shuddered and gave it back.

"Let's hope we don't need a new roof or anything this year," she said.

"Let's hope we don't even need to buy *gas*," her father said. "Or food."

Emily hadn't even thought about how much all of this special veterinary care must have cost, and now she felt guilty. "I'm sorry," she said. "Was it really, really expensive?"

Her father grinned. "Put it this way, Em. I hope you aren't going to need braces. And college is out, too."

Oh, no. Emily was about to offer to give up her allowance—for the next several *years*—when her mother shook her head.

"Don't tease her, Theo," her mother said, and turned around in her seat to look at her. "Are you happy?"

Incredibly happy. Emily nodded.

"Okay, then," her mother said. "I can't think of a better way to spend our money. Now, please, put on your seat belt."

Emily quickly pulled her seat belt across herself and clicked it in place. She would have liked to belt Zack in somehow, too, but he was sprawled out across the rest of the seat, with his muzzle resting on her knee, and she didn't want to disturb him. "Um, thank you," she said. "I mean, really. *Thank you.*"

Her father nodded. "You're welcome. But no birthday presents. And nothing for Hanukkah or Christmas, either. And—"

"Knock it off, buddy," her mother said, with a grin. "*Drive.*"

Her father grinned back, saluted her, and started the car.

When they pulled up to the house, their next-door neighbor, Mrs. Peabody, was lifting some groceries out of her car. She stopped, set the bags down on the hood, and walked over to meet them.

"So, this must be the famous Zack," she said.

Since he had technically washed up on the Peabodys' rocks, Emily and her parents had told them all about it, the first time they had run into them afterwards.

"Yes, this is Zack," Emily said, feeling very proud.

The dog wagged his tail at Mrs. Peabody in a friendly way.

"Well, now, he's going to be *something*, isn't he," Mrs. Peabody said, and patted him briefly, before going back to retrieve her groceries.

Even in such a short period of time, the dog's fur was already growing back, and looked thick and fluffy. When he was strong enough, he was going to need a bath, because there were some stains in the white fur, but he still looked good. His legs and tail were gracefully feathered, and his brown eyes were so dark that they looked almost black. He was also starting to gain a little weight, and wasn't nearly as frail as he had been just a few days earlier.

Zack seemed to want to explore everything at

once, and Emily let him wander around the yard for a few minutes before steering him over towards the deck and the back door.

When they went inside, Josephine was sitting on the kitchen floor, washing her face. As soon as she saw the dog, her fur puffed up and she hissed, before leaping dramatically up onto the kitchen table.

Zack just stood near the door, waving his tail pleasantly.

Emily didn't want her cat to feel jealous, or left out, so she went over to pick her up and hug her.

"You're still the best cat in the world," she said. "We just have a dog now, too, that's all."

Josephine hissed again, but she was also purring, so Emily figured that the hissing was mostly just for show.

The dog wandered around the kitchen for a moment, sniffing everything, and accepted a Milk-Bone Emily's father offered him, although he didn't eat it. Instead, he stood in the middle of the floor, looking bemused and uncertain, and holding the biscuit in his mouth.

Emily felt a little unsure of herself, too. She had expected the dog to be overjoyed to be in his new house, but so far, he mostly seemed—uncomfortable. Anxious. Shy, even.

"What do we do now?" she asked.

"You both relax, that's what you do," her mother said. "This is a big change for him, all at once, Em. He needs a little time to adjust."

Emily nodded, but she was still uneasy. Was there some trick to having a dog that she didn't know about? He wasn't healthy enough to do things like chase after balls and Frisbees yet, so they couldn't just start playing around and having fun. So what should they do, instead?

Maybe he was tired. Now that she thought about it, *she* was pretty tired. It had been a really long week.

"Well, I don't know about the rest of you," her father said, "but I'm going to go read the paper." He reached down to tap Zack—tentatively—on the head. "Um, good boy. We're glad to have you here."

Her father *always* read the paper in the morning, so that seemed nice and normal. "Maybe I should show him where his room is," Emily said to her mother.

Her mother nodded. "Sure. We really don't have anything planned for today, so I think we should all just take it easy. Maybe we can watch a movie or something later, but that's about it."

"Okay, that'd be good," Emily said. She still felt sort of formal, and strange, but decided that she would head for her room and see if the dog followed her. "Come on, Zack, let's go upstairs."

He immediately fell in right behind her, although she paused to let him go first on the stairs, so she could make sure that it wasn't too hard for him. He lifted his cast for a few seconds, and then hung back.

"Come on, boy," she said encouragingly.

Zack started to lift himself onto the first step, and then retreated, holding his cast in the air.

She had never really noticed how *steep* the stairs were. And since he was injured, she should have realized that he wasn't going to be able to make his way up there anytime soon. So, they were going to have to think of a new plan. It was a good thing she and her father had made that extra dog bed, after all.

"I'm sorry, Zack, we'll stay down here," she said. "But, just so you'll know, that's Mom and Dad's room," Emily said, pointing towards the second floor. "And that's the guest room and the upstairs office. Mom likes to work in there, but Dad usually works in the den. If you go down the other way, that's the bathroom, and that's my room, over there."

The dog seemed to take all of that in, although she couldn't be sure. Besides, it wasn't as though he was going to be *quizzed* on it later.

She guided him into the den, where Josephine was already stretched out in the cardboard bed, taking up a lot more room than an eight-pound cat *should* be able to take up. Emily patted the towels, to indicate that Zack should lie down there, but the dog looked wary and kept his distance.

Josephine stretched luxuriously, taking up even *more* room.

"No, come on," Emily said, picking her up and moving her over onto the couch.

Josephine jumped off the couch right away, and went to lie on top of the television, instead. That wasn't ideal, but at least it meant that she wouldn't get in Zack's way. It was kind of funny that a small cat could intimidate a dog who weighed ten times more than she did.

The dog was still standing there, with his Milk-Bone in his mouth, and Emily suddenly felt really, really tired. But then, she knew, just as suddenly, that she was fine and the *dog* was the one who was tired. Which was weird—*again*—but, it was probably just because they had been spending so much time together, and she was starting to understand the way he reacted to things.

"Okay, you really should lie down now," she said. "Stay here for a minute, I'll be right back."

She hurried out to the kitchen to get his blue dishes, and brought them into the den. She set the water dish near the bed, and put some dry food in the other dish, in case he was hungry, too.

"There you go," she said. "Now, you're all set. Lie down now, okay?"

The dog climbed carefully into the cardboard bed—but still didn't lie down.

He wasn't due for any more medication for a few hours, but maybe his lungs hurt? So she tapped his chest for a couple of minutes, doing the coupage she had been taught.

The dog's tail wagged, but he stayed on his feet.

All right, she was running out of ideas. Maybe it would help if she stretched out on the floor next to his bed? If he thought she was going to rest, maybe he would decide to try it, too.

Her new school had emailed out a list of books they wanted all of the incoming seventh graders to read during the summer, and she was way behind. So she went back upstairs and selected one from the pile on her desk. Once she was in the den again—where the dog was still standing uncertainly on top of the folded towels—she grabbed a throw pillow from the couch and lay down on the floor.

Zack promptly climbed out of his cardboard bed,

curled up next to her legs, crunched his Milk-Bone, and let out a contented sigh.

Josephine jumped over from the television, peered at him suspiciously—and then got back into the cardboard bed, seeming to fall asleep within seconds.

Emily had every intention of reading industriously, but there was something very peaceful about being surrounded by sleeping pets, especially when they both seemed to be so happy. So what would it hurt if she took a little nap, too, even though they were all on the *floor*?

Just for ten minutes, twenty at the most.

Or an hour.

Tops.

15

She must have been more tired than she realized, because she slept through lunch and then most of the afternoon. Her mother had obviously decided that she needed the extra rest, because she didn't wake her up until right before supper. But she must have come in at some point earlier, because Emily was surprised to find herself covered with an old quilt her great-aunt had made out of leftover pieces of colorful material.

"You all seemed so peaceful that I didn't have the heart to wake you up," her mother said. "But it looked so *uncomfortable*."

A little, maybe. Next time, she would have to see if Zack maybe felt strong enough to get up on the couch or something. "Kind of, yeah," Emily said, and yawned as she sat up. "What time is it?"

"Almost five-thirty," her mother said. "We didn't feel like cooking, so your father went to get some take-out. He should be back any minute now. It's so nice out that we're going to eat on the deck."

Emily nodded, patting Zack and Josephine—who were also yawning, and then ran upstairs to get washed up. Zack waited patiently for her at the bottom of the steps, looking very relieved when she returned.

Her father came home with Mexican food, which was generally a good choice, because there were so many different vegetarian options, even if the food itself wasn't necessarily all that authentic. Thai and Indian food also worked out pretty well, most of the time. They almost never ordered Chinese food, because her father always said there was *no such thing* as decent Chinese food in Maine. Emily was pretty sure that her mother felt the exact same way about all Mexican restaurants that weren't in California—or Mexico itself, but other than an occasional muttered "The plate is very *hot*" comment, she wasn't inclined to go on and on about it, the way Emily's father did. Although Emily had noticed that waiters actually *did* always say that, right before serving the food at really bad Mexican restaurants. Lobster houses and fish restaurants were usually a problem, because they might have *one* chicken dish, or a hamburger, on the menu, and so the only thing Emily could order would be salad and bread.

As they sat out on the deck, they could see sailboats gliding home for the night, and bulkier motor boats and lobster boats puttering along. Seagulls, as always, swarmed around the lobster boats, looking for food. A few kayaks went by, too—one of the men waving at them, since he was in her mother's racing club, and they even saw a canoe with two people paddling efficiently in the bow and the stern.

"Did you go out today?" Emily asked her mother.

Her mother nodded, helping herself to some guacamole and adding both chipotle chile powder and Tabasco sauce to it. "For about an hour. I felt a little rusty."

With all of the time they had spent at the animal hospital for the past week, her mother had skipped quite a few of her regular training sessions.

"Tomorrow, I'm going to go out early," her mother said, and made a "those awful tourists!" gesture towards the water. "When it's nice and quiet."

"It won't be quiet until after Labor Day," her father said, in a grumpy "when will the tourists ever *leave*?" voice.

Emily grinned, since her parents said some version of those remarks every single day during the summer—just the way everyone else in Maine did. Zack was lying next to her feet, and she cut off a piece of cheese enchilada, to see if he would like it.

"Hold it right there," her father said instantly. "Are you going to make a habit of sneaking him food under the table?"

Emily paused, her hand in mid-air, Zack's ears going up as the scent of cheese caught his attention. "I'm not sneaking anything, Dad," she said. "I'm doing it right in front of you."

"Oh." He frowned. "Well, okay, that's true, but it wasn't really my point."

She couldn't *not* give it to Zack, after he'd already zeroed in on the piece of food. "I'm not going to make him all rude and begging. But he's had a hard time. He should get *treats*." Lots of them, in fact.

Her mother frowned, too. "All right. But, if he starts behaving badly at meals, we're going to say, 'I told you so.'"

Coming from her mother, that was pretty fierce, even though it was kind of harmless, as threats went. Emily wanted to pretend to shudder, and say "*Oooh*," but that was the sort of sarcastic response that might actually make her parents mad—and she usually tried to avoid that, if possible. "Okay," she said instead. "That sounds scary."

"As it was meant to," her mother said, and nodded once for emphasis.

They caught her giving Zack food two more times during the meal, but they couldn't really criticize her for it, because her mother had also absentmindedly handed him a corn chip at one point.

After dinner, Emily took Zack for a careful walk around the yard, watching to make sure that his breathing was smooth and easy. Then, her mother supervised as she gave him his evening antibiotics and other medications, including the special vitamins Dr. Kasanofsky prescribed. She had thought it might be hard to give him his medicine, but Zack would wag his tail the whole time, especially if she put the pills in a little piece of cheese or something first.

Then, she went up to get her laptop and bring it down to the den—while Zack waited at the bottom of the stairs, so that she could check her email and maybe even call a couple of her friends. She had been so tired all week whenever they got home from the vet's that she felt like she hadn't spoken to any of them in *months*, and it was strange to be so out of touch.

She had three different main groups of friends, who didn't really overlap. First, there were all of her friends from her elementary school. Bobby was her best friend from school, since she had known him for so long, and they hung out constantly, but her other closest school friends were Harriet and Florence. Harriet was really smart and was totally into science and math, and Florence was tiny, but played just about every single sport in the *world*—and played them incredibly aggressively, too. She was especially good at hockey and downhill skiing.

Her second group of friends were all of the kids she knew whose parents taught at the college. Most of them lived in Brunswick or Bath, and went to different schools, but there was so much social stuff through the college that Emily had gotten to know them at her swimming lessons, and museum events, and department parties, and stuff like that. Her very *best* friend was Karen, whose father was a music professor, while her mother was a painter. Karen loved music, too, and could play the piano, the cello, the saxophone, *and* the flute.

Sometimes, Emily kind of wished that she and

her parents had a house right in town, near the college, because there was always so much more going on there. It wasn't that they lived that far away, but sometimes, it *felt* far, because they had to drive to get anywhere.

Then again, it was pretty hard to complain about living right on the water. It just happened that her neighborhood was almost all retired people or summer houses. If it weren't for Bobby and his sister and brother, she would have been the only person under *forty* on their section of the peninsula.

Her third group of friends was—well—everyone else. Her father was Jewish, but he really didn't practice anymore, so they went to an Episcopal church, because her mother liked it. Because of that, she had friends from Sunday school. She also had friends from some of the day camps she had gone to over the years—art camp, sailing camp, nature camp, *and* computer camp. She didn't get to see them as much as she saw her other friends, but they spent a lot of time online, and emailed and IM'd each other and all. Her cousins—she had five—lived in New York and California, and *they* all stayed in touch online, too.

It had been kind of funny, about six months earlier, when her parents had asked her if she would ever go anywhere near a social-networking site, apparently assuming that the answer would be "no, of course not, *never* in a million years." They had been pretty horrified when she told them she had profiles on two different sites.

She wasn't *stupid* about being online, so her profiles were set to private, and only her actual friends could see them. And if a stranger wanted to friend her, she always just declined the invitation. Her parents had insisted upon checking this for themselves, and they had all ended up having a pretty big argument, because Emily thought that was a *total* invasion of privacy. It wasn't like she and her friends were doing anything *bad*, but she still didn't particularly want to have her parents reading over her shoulder.

And, predictably, when she saw some of the postings on her wall, her mother *did* comment on their grammar, punctuation, and abbreviations, not seeming to realize that one of the reasons that she and her friends used stuff like "BRB" and "OMG" and "LOL" was *just to annoy adults*.

Her father had set up some complicated parental control software on her computer, but then he had gotten confused about how to make it work, and Emily had had to show him how to configure it and all. Which, they had both agreed, kind of defeated the purpose of the software entirely, so they uninstalled it.

Their final compromise was that she had—reluctantly—friended one of her aunts, who was now, she assumed, keeping an eye on her, although mostly they just sent each other funny videos and stuff. Her parents were always saying that *nothing* online was really private, even if it seemed that way, and that she had to be very, very careful. To make them happy, Emily had promised never to post or email anything that might keep her from getting into college or running for any important political offices—even though she wasn't completely sure exactly what would fall into that category.

So, anyway, she sprawled out on the floor in the den and answered emails and chatted with her friends for a while, until her father came in to see if she wanted to watch a movie. Her mother made popcorn and lemonade, and they all sat together on the couch while Zack slept in the cardboard bed.

"Pretty nice day," her father remarked, as the movie started.

Emily nodded.

It had been a *great* day.

16

Her mother had said that she absolutely couldn't sleep on the floor all night, and made up the couch for her. But it was too high for Zack to climb up, so they rolled out a sleeping bag, instead. The floor was kind of hard, but Emily was tired, and had no trouble at all falling asleep.

After lunch the next day, Bobby rode his bike over so that he could meet Zack. Her mother agreed that they could take him for a real walk, and not just around the yard, as long as they promised not to go too far.

"Let's walk up to Mrs. Griswold's house," Bobby suggested.

Bobby *always* wanted to walk by Mrs. Griswold's house, because he thought it was funny when she came out and yelled at them.

"Why make her mad, if we don't have to?" Emily asked.

Bobby shrugged. "She might not even see us.

Besides, we live here, too, so we can walk wherever we want."

Emily still didn't think it was such a hot idea, but they wandered up the dirt road in that direction. It was pretty hot out, and humid enough so that they walked slowly.

"Have you done any of the summer reading?" Emily asked.

Bobby shook his head.

"Are you going to?" Emily asked.

Bobby thought about that, and then shook his head. "Nope. Or, I don't know, maybe just one of them. Besides, they all look wicked boring."

His parents were a lot less strict than hers, because she had already read six of the books on the list, and had promised to finish at least four more before the first day of school. Bobby always said that it didn't matter, because the only thing he wanted to do when he grew up was to work on his father's boat, but Emily had always suspected that he privately liked school a lot more than he wanted to admit.

They were a few hundred yards away from the house, when the dog suddenly seemed to be worn out. He was favoring his hip much more than he had been, and his tail was hanging instead of waving. He was also starting to pant.

"I don't think he was ready yet," Emily said, feeling guilty. "We'd better take him home right away."

Bobby nodded. "Do we carry him?"

Not likely. Even malnourished, he was a *big* dog. Emily shook her head. "I think he's too heavy, and we might hurt him by accident. Maybe if we just rest here for a while, and then go back?"

Bobby nodded, and they sat down on the shoulder of the road. Naturally, they were almost exactly across from Mrs. Griswold's house—which was a weathered cottage, with grey shingles and a big front porch—but, until Zack felt better, they didn't have much choice.

Zack lay down next to Emily, resting his muzzle on her leg. And he must have been *really* tired, because he fell asleep immediately.

Emily gestured towards the house with her chin. "What are we going to do if she comes out?" Since normally, they just ran away.

"Dunno," Bobby said, and paused. "It's probably not true that she keeps a really big gun by the door."

Probably? Emily looked at him uneasily. "Who said that?"

Bobby shrugged. "Larry." Larry was his big brother, who had just turned seventeen. "He said she fired it at him one time, and there was all this buckshot everywhere, and he could have *died*."

With all of the scary things people said about Mrs. Griswold, she could believe it—except that Larry always told Bobby completely exaggerated stories, and Bobby was gullible enough to believe every word.

"I don't think she has a gun," Emily said. Although lots of people in Maine did own guns—mostly for hunting, so she might really have one. "And even if she does, she wouldn't *shoot* it at us."

Or, anyway, she hoped not.

Bobby looked uneasily across the road at the house, which was surrounded by a three-foot-high white wooden fence. "I think she would. And she totally hates dogs, even more than she hates *kids*."

That probably was true, because Emily had heard that she always called the police when the Nickersons' Jack Russell terrier, whose name was Wanda, barked too much.

"So, wait," she said. "*Why* did we walk up this way again?"

"Because it seemed like it would be really funny," Bobby said.

Emily nodded. "Oh, okay. Good idea."

They sat there, looking at the quiet house.

"You *know* she killed her husband," Bobby said.

No, she knew that was the *rumor* around town. Emily shook her head. "My parents said it was a car accident." And she was *pretty* sure that it was true.

"*Maybe*," Bobby said ominously. Then, his expression brightened. "Hey, I know what to do! What about your wagon? Is it still in the garage?"

They hadn't used the wagon for years, but since her parents tended to let things pile up in there, she was pretty sure it was somewhere among the clutter. "That's a good idea," Emily said. "Then, we could just pull him home."

"Okay." Bobby got up, with dirt all over his jeans—none of which he brushed off. "I'll go get it."

"Thanks," Emily said, although it was a little creepy to think of sitting in front of Mrs. Griswold's house *all by herself*. Even though she wasn't a murderer.

Probably.

Bobby nodded, and started jogging down the road.

While she and Zack waited, Emily rested a soothing hand on his back.

"I'm sorry. I didn't know you would get so tired," she said. "I'll be more careful next time."

Zack wagged his tail, without opening his eyes,

and she hoped that he understood what she had said. He always seemed really smart, though, so she assumed that, at the very least, he knew that she was apologizing.

But, the truth was, if she were being completely honest with herself, she would admit that whatever Zack was, it went beyond being *smart*. Too often, it felt as though he could read her mind—*really* read her mind—and that she could read *his*. She wasn't doing it on purpose, and the whole idea was sort of unsettling, but it just seemed to happen.

Over and over.

And now, it was maybe happening again, because he had opened his eyes and was looking at her intently.

Unless it was her imagination. Yeah, it had to be her imagination. Nothing else made sense.

"I mean, they say dogs know stuff," she said to him. "Like, when their owners are coming home and everything, dogs just figure it out. So, I'm sure it's just normal intuition, right?"

Zack cocked his head to one side, looking directly at her.

She had seen a cartoon once, where the dog seemed to be listening, but just heard gibberish, except whenever the person said the dog's name. So, maybe people just *thought* dogs knew more than they really did. Like, it was just—well, she couldn't remember the word for it, but she knew there *was* a word.

Or maybe dogs *did* know almost everything, but because they couldn't speak, there was no way of proving it. She never really had the same feeling with Josephine, but cats were different, and probably cared more about keeping their privacy. Josephine did, anyway. As far as Emily could tell, her cat liked to be mysterious and sly—and go out of her way to startle people, just for the fun of it.

That very morning, her father had been making crabmeat omelets—yuck—as well as a cheese, onion, and mushroom one for her, and when he'd offered a bit of crabmeat to Zack, Emily had heard herself saying, "No, he doesn't like fish." Her father had shrugged and given him a piece of cheese, instead—but Emily just sat there and wondered why she had been so utterly sure that that was true. Her parents were distracted, and didn't notice, which was probably good, because she had no idea how she would explain it.

Bobby was still nowhere in sight, and she glanced down at Zack.

"*Do* you like fish?" she asked. "To eat, I mean?"

Zack didn't move, but she would have sworn that she caught a powerful whiff of raw, rotting fish. It smelled sort of the way a boat smelled, after the fishermen and women unloaded their catch, and before they hosed everything down. It was sort of like the time she had thought she was smelling strong floor cleaner, but it turned out to be what the medicine in the nebulizer in the back room at the animal hospital smelled like, instead.

Okay, there was unquestionably something going on here. The fact that she wasn't quite sure what it *was* didn't mean that—

Just then, she saw a curtain move in the front room window, and then, the door of the grey house flew open.

Mrs. Griswold was coming outside!

17

Mrs. Griswold might have been tall once, but as long as Emily had known her, she had been hunched over a cane. She was probably in her early sixties, but it was hard to be sure. Her hair was closer to white than grey and was almost always piled up messily underneath a floppy, beige fishing hat, complete with homemade lures. Mrs. Griswold was the kind of person who *always* wore a sweater, no matter how warm it was, and was—even by crusty New Englander standards—considered "peculiar." As far as Emily was concerned, she was just *mean*—and really weird, too.

"What's all this?" Mrs. Griswold demanded. "Why are you sitting there staring at my house?"

"I-I'm sorry," Emily said quickly, as the woman came barreling down her front walk towards them, making remarkably good time on her cane. "My dog got a little bit tired. We're just, um—we're about to leave."

Zack got up and waved his tail charmingly.

Mrs. Griswold narrowed her eyes—surprisingly clear blue eyes—at him. "Since when do you people have a dog?"

"Um, since—" Emily felt so nervous that she couldn't remember. "I'm not sure. Just, you know, recently."

Mrs. Griswold scowled at both of them. "Well, I had better not hear that animal barking. I don't like to be disturbed."

Emily was much too polite to say "yeah, no kidding," but she *did* think it. "No, ma'am. He won't."

They looked at each other uncomfortably, but also not without some mutual hostility.

"Go on with you now," Mrs. Griswold said crossly. "I can't hear myself think, with you out here watching like this."

Emily, for one, did not need to be told twice. "Come on, boy," she said, and led him down the road towards her house.

Zack followed her amiably enough, but she saw him look back a couple of times, obviously curious.

It was a big relief to see Bobby heading in their direction, dragging the red metal wagon along behind him. Since he was so much heavier now, because of eating regular meals, it was kind of a production to get Zack up *into* it. It was great that he wasn't as thin and bony as he had been even a couple of days earlier, but, it *did* make him more difficult to lift.

"Why didn't you guys wait for me?" Bobby asked, looking disappointed. "I came back like, as fast as I could."

"Mrs. Griswold came out," Emily said, and couldn't hold back a shiver.

Bobby's eyes widened. "Wow, did she throw anything at you?"

Emily shook her head. "I think she maybe wanted to, but she just told us she didn't want us in front of her house, so we left."

"Did she scream and shake her fist?" Bobby asked.

Emily shook her head. "Not really. She was just—cross."

"Did she have her gun?" he asked.

Since she figured he was kidding, Emily nodded. "Yeah. It was *huge*. Like in the movies."

Bobby's eyes widened even more.

"I'm kidding," she said.

He blushed, but nodded. "Yup. Knew you were."

Maybe.

Once he was finally in the wagon, Zack seemed

to like his new perch very much, lounging there quite regally. His cast was casually propped up on the side of the wagon, and he had stopped panting. His tail was dangling over the edge, and she picked it up, tucking it inside the wagon so that it wouldn't get caught in the wheels.

"He looks pretty happy," Bobby said. "Maybe we should take him for a little ride."

Emily nodded, since Zack seemed positively delighted to be sitting in the wagon, and no longer tired at all. "Sure, why not? We haven't been able to explore much, and he's probably curious about what's around here."

So they pulled him almost all the way up to the access road, before turning around to go back. Her mother called her cell phone at one point, to ask why they weren't home yet, and when Emily explained, her mother laughed and said that they should go ahead and give him the grand tour.

Zack really seemed to enjoy trundling along— even though the ride must be pretty bumpy. He looked around attentively at everything they passed, almost as though he was taking mental notes about the entire neighborhood.

Then again, there wasn't *that* much to show him. This part of the peninsula was narrow, so they could see the water on both sides of the road. Except for a huge ultra-modern mansion that had been built by summer people who visited maybe two weekends a year, the houses were mostly on the small side, and surrounded by pine trees. The dirt road itself was very sunny, and dry enough to be dusty, but most of the houses were in the shade. The lots were pretty far apart, and the area was wooded enough so that each home seemed quite private.

Most of the houses had docks, and at least half of them had sailboats or motorboats anchored nearby. Dr. Henrik, who had taught geology at the college before he retired, waved at them from his *really* impressive English flower garden, and they waved back.

"Fine dog you have there, Emily!" he called. "Your father told me all about it, down at the store."

"Thank you!" Emily called back. "His name's Zachary."

Dr. Henrik nodded approvingly. "Excellent choice. Very dignified. I'll be sure to tell everyone when I go down to get the evening edition."

Obviously, there was more than one store in town, but everyone in this part of Bailey's Cove always bought their milk and newspapers and other necessities at Cyril's Mini-Mart. Cyril had run the little store for years, and *looked* like he was about a hundred and twenty, although he ran around like he was only—eighty or so. The rumor around town was that he never actually slept, because the store *always* seemed to be open, even during the middle of hurricanes and blizzards. Cyril liked everyone, except tourists, Mrs. Griswold—and Bobby.

"Want to go down and say hi to Cyril?" Emily asked.

"Ha," Bobby said, and made a face.

When he was about six years old, Bobby had tried to shoplift a Snickers bar from the front counter, and Cyril had never forgiven him. For that matter, Cyril always referred to Bobby's father as "that lousy roughneck punk," because when he was about the same age, *he* had stolen—and promptly eaten—a piece of red licorice from the penny candy section. Because of that, Cyril described Bobby's entire family as being "bad to the bone."

But Cyril loved hockey more than anything, and Emily had learned that the best way to get along with him was to say, "How are those Black Bears doing, sir?" every time she saw him. Asking about the Portland Pirates or Boston Bruins worked pretty well, too. He didn't care much about the Bowdoin Polar Bears, but since she was a faculty child, he was polite about that and pretended to find them interesting, too.

A couple of cars were coming down the road, and they moved the wagon safely off to the side, waiting for them to go by. One of them was being driven by Kurt, who sometimes hauled traps for Bobby's father, and he beeped the horn once at them as he passed. The other car was going very slowly, and ended up stopping about a hundred feet away.

Some people who were obviously tourists—it was always easy to tell, from the souvenir t-shirts they were inclined to wear, to the delighted "isn't New England *adorable*" expressions they often had on their faces—got out. A man in a brand-new, very stiff, perfectly clean Red Sox cap stayed behind the wheel, while two women in impractical shoes and a man with a fancy camera that would have made Emily's father *drool* walked over.

"Look at that," one of the women said to the other. "That is *so* Maine."

Bobby raised his eyebrows at Emily, who shrugged a "yeah, whatever, just humor them" at him.

"Can I take your picture?" the man with the camera asked.

Emily and Bobby posed politely, and even Zack's

143

posture seemed to improve at once. The man walked back and forth to select the best angle and then snapped off a rapid series of photos. Emily managed not to cringe at the careless way he was swinging the camera and super-fancy lens around, not even *supporting* it properly, or wearing the strap around his neck. Had her father witnessed the scene, he might have fainted dead away.

It went without saying that everyone in Maine—not just Cyril—complained year-round about tourists, even though Emily's mother sometimes pointed out at town council meetings and other gatherings that they *did* contribute a lot to the state's economy. Most locals would say something like, "Well, Joanne, you're not a native; you just don't understand." Her parents had lived in Maine for almost twenty years now, but a lot of people still thought of them as being newcomers. Since her father had a little bit of a New York accent, he was *always* described by people as being "from away."

"Such a beautiful day," one of the women said. She was wearing a big straw hat with flowers and a striped ribbon on it, while the other woman had settled for oversized yellow sunglasses.

"A-yuh," Bobby said, with such a perfect accent that Emily had to bite her lip not to crack up.

Tourists were pretty sure that people in Maine always said "A-yuh" instead of "Yes."

"We're trying to find Crowley's Sea Shack," the woman in the hat said. "We asked the man at the general store, but he didn't seem to know where it was."

That meant that Cyril must be in an unusually good mood. When he was cranky, he liked to send tourists miles *away* from things. Anyway, Crowley's was a famous local restaurant, which specialized in lobster and fried clams served on paper plates.

"Cawn't git there from he-ah," Bobby said.

This time, Emily had to fight even harder not to laugh, since he'd just used about four different accents—Boston, Southern, Maine, and a dash of Harvard—in a single sentence.

"Hmmm." The woman in the sunglasses frowned. "I'll go ask my husband to check the GPS."

"There's some folks, near the end a this he-ah road, sell the best lobsters Down East," Bobby said, just as helpful as can be. "Think they go by the name of Percival, and I reckon they might be able to steer you right."

Emily grinned, since he was talking about his parents. Bobby's father sold most of his haul commercially, but he and Mrs. Percival also ran a small lobster pound of their own for locals, to make extra money.

"Thank you," the other woman said, and then smiled at Emily. "Are you enjoying your time out of the city? It's so peaceful up here."

Bobby looked baffled, but it wasn't the first time people had jumped to incorrect conclusions about her—and it wouldn't be the last.

Unfortunately.

And it never got any less upsetting, even when the person was well-meaning. Maybe even *especially* when the person was well-meaning.

It wasn't going to help to lose her temper, so Emily just nodded. "I know. The Fresh Air Fund has been *so good* to me."

Now, Bobby looked even more confused.

But the woman was nodding, too. "Yes, it's a wonderful program." Then, she reached out to pat Zack, who stiffened and leaned away from her. The woman hesitated, then withdrew her hand. "What a cute dog. How did he get injured?"

"Gang warfare" was probably the answer she wanted to hear. "He got caught in the cross-fire," Emily said, very politely. "It was awful."

"Yes, it must have been," the woman said, her

expression full of sympathy. "What a blessing that he's okay."

"Rachel, Gordon thinks he knows the directions now," the other woman called over.

"Okay, good." The woman in the hat smiled at them. "Enjoy the rest of your summer!"

Once the tourists were gone, Emily folded her arms tightly and took a couple of deep breaths.

Zack made an anxious little sound, and she unfolded her arms long enough to pat him on the head. He wagged his tail, in a relieved sort of way, but still seemed to be uneasy.

"What was *that* all about?" Bobby asked.

For a really smart kid, a fair amount of stuff went right over Bobby's head. Or maybe he just had a different kind of radar entirely. She wasn't sure if she'd been born with it, or learned it by experience—or both, but she definitely had radar. Plenty of it. "I'm black," Emily said.

Bobby shrugged. "Okay. Thanks for letting me know."

"So, if I'm in Maine," Emily said, "that must mean that some nice country family took me in for the summer. You know, to get me out of my deprived, inner-city neighborhood."

Bobby stared at her. "No way."

Emily nodded.

Catching on completely now, Bobby's mouth dropped open. "But—that's *prejudiced*!"

Emily shrugged. One of the expressions she'd heard people use was "death by a thousand cuts," and it was a pretty accurate description. "I don't think she meant it that way. It was just, you know, her automatic thought."

"Wow," Bobby said, and shook his head with disgust. "That stinks."

Yeah. It really did.

18

When they got back to her house, she and Bobby didn't discuss the tourists again, because there really wasn't any point. But playing with the Wii for a while made them both relax, and definitely helped cheer her up. Zack didn't know what to make of a game that caused people to jump wildly around a room, waving little plastic boxes, and he barked a few times to express this.

Her mother invited Bobby to stay for supper, but his family was going over to his uncle's house later, and he headed home, instead. Since it was so hot out, her mother decided that rather than cooking a big, heavy meal, they should have a tossed salad, with lots of fresh vegetables and greens, plus tuna fish for her parents, and a big scoop of egg salad for Emily. Sometimes, just for fun, they made fake egg salad with tofu and turmeric and all, but tonight, her mother was making the real thing, with lots of onions, pickles, and celery salt.

149

After dinner, Emily helped her father with the dishes, while her mother went upstairs to work for a while. When they had finished cleaning up, Emily considered going online, but she didn't really feel like it. The two tense encounters this afternoon had left her sort of edgy, and maybe even out-of-sorts, and she wanted to burn off a little energy. Sitting behind her laptop and firing off IMs right and left was fun and all, but it was—passive.

So she took Zack for a short walk around the yard, and then flopped down on one of the deck chairs to look up at the sky. It was still pretty hot, but it was a clear night, and there were lots of stars out.

Zack climbed up—laboriously—onto the deck chair, too, and she had to move her legs to make room for him. Even though it had only been a couple of days, it was hard to remember what it was like *not* to have a dog. It would be nice if Josephine could hang around outside *with* them, but she was an indoors cat and it wouldn't be safe for her. Besides, Emily could see her sitting in her bedroom window, and she looked quite content—and superior—up there.

She had been outside for quite a while when the back door opened, and her father came out onto the deck.

"Ah, there you are," he said. "I was starting to get worried that the two of you hadn't come back yet."

"It's nice out tonight," Emily said. "I didn't really want to come indoors right away."

Her father nodded, and lay back on one of the other lawn chairs.

They listened to small waves breaking against the rocks, the chirp of crickets, and the occasional passing car.

"You've been awfully quiet tonight," he said. "Is everything okay?"

"Sure," Emily said, although she must have tensed, because Zachary lifted his head anxiously.

"So, nothing's wrong?" her father asked.

Emily shook her head. But she knew he didn't believe her, and—since it also wasn't true—she let out her breath. "Mrs. Griswold yelled at me this afternoon, because Zack had to take a rest when we were walking, and it happened to be in front of her house."

He sighed. "Well, she's—cantankerous."

Which was the kind of word Emily liked, because it was easy to tell what it meant, even if it was unfamiliar. She happened to *know* this one—but it wouldn't have mattered if she hadn't.

"I'm sorry if it upset you," he said. "Try not to

151

take her too seriously. She just likes to go her own way."

Or, maybe, she just liked to be nasty to people. But Emily nodded, looking at a small bright flicker in the sky, and wondering if it was just a plane, or something more interesting than that, like a shooting star. Zack had settled back down, and she started some very light coupage on his chest, since she was supposed to do it at least four times a day, and had only done it three times so far today.

"You're still pretty quiet, Em," her father said, after a minute. "Is that all that's bothering you?"

No. She didn't want to bring it up, though, because he might get upset, or—potentially even worse—*outraged*.

"Did you and Bobby quarrel?" he asked.

She shook her head. They didn't argue very often, but when she and Bobby *did*, it was usually a nasty one, and involved not speaking for a few days, after which they would make up, and promise never, ever, ever to let it happen again.

Another boat was moving past them out in the sound, but all they could see was a faint silhouette, and its night running lights.

"Am I from the inner city?" Emily asked.

Her father must not have expected anything

like that, because he sat up, looking startled. "What do you mean?"

"Was that where I was born?" she asked.

It took a very long time for her father to answer.

"No," he said.

It had been a closed adoption, so Emily really didn't know much of *anything* about where she had been born—or, when it came right down to it, who she was. She had a birthday, of course—September 18—but she wasn't even sure if that was her *real* birthday, or one her parents had picked out so that she would feel normal.

Her mother never minded talking about it, but the entire subject of her adoption made her father almost as uncomfortable as it made her, so they rarely brought it up. But even her mother had never really given her many specific details, other than to say that her birth mother had loved her enough to make sure that she would grow up in the most loving home she could find, and how lucky they were to have her. Emily assumed that her parents knew a lot more than they were willing—or legally able—to tell her. The technical term was actually a "semi-open adoption," but she, personally, didn't know much of anything at all. She'd also never gotten a birthday present or a Christmas card or a photograph or any other indication that either of her birth parents ever thought about her at all.

She knew one other adopted kid, Maryann, who was from China and was a couple of years older than she was. Their parents—Maryann's mother was an adjunct European lecturer at the college— had made a point of trying to get them together regularly, but as it turned out, she and Maryann had absolutely nothing else in common and never did much more than say, "oh, yeah, hi," if they happened to run into each other.

"Is September eighteenth my real birthday?" she asked.

Her father nodded. "Of course."

"I mean, my *real* birthday," she said, "and not one you and Mom gave me so that I'd feel, you know, more grounded."

Her father let out his breath. "It's your real birthday," he said quietly. "You were only about a week old when we brought you home."

Okay, that was good. And it was a much more definite piece of information than they usually told her.

"Want me to go get your mother?" her father asked.

Emily looked up. Sometimes, her father liked to

avoid potentially complicated conversations like this, by mumbling that he needed to go get some work done or something. "You don't want to talk about it with me?"

"I think she would want to discuss it *with* us," he said.

But then, it might turn into a much bigger deal than she wanted it to be, and there were too many questions they couldn't answer, anyway, so they would all end up getting frustrated. And she never wanted them to think that she wished she had different parents or anything like that—because it wasn't true. Supposedly, when she turned eighteen, she might be allowed to petition the court for more information, but that was a *long* time away.

Her father stood up. "Look, I'll be right back, and then the three of us can all—"

"No, it's not that important, I just—" Emily shook her head. Zack had snuggled up a little closer to her during all of this, and she was reminded—again—of how incredibly nice it was to have a dog. "Well, there was a lady today."

Her father hesitated, but sat back down. "What lady?" he asked carefully. Nervously, even.

Emily shrugged. "Just a lady. They were, like, you know, tourists. They asked Bobby and me how to get to Crowley's, because I guess Cyril wouldn't tell them."

Her father nodded.

"And she thought I was lucky to be visiting Maine and getting to spend time in the country," Emily said. "You know, like I was deprived and some charity had to send me up here."

Her father sighed. "People make stupid assumptions sometimes, Emily. I wish they didn't."

Yeah. "But, isn't that kind of what happened?" Emily said. "I mean, that you and Mom were really nice, and took me, because my parents—uh, you know, birth parents—couldn't, or *wouldn't*—or whatever—take care of me?"

Her father looked a little bit like he wanted to run away, or at least go find her mother as quickly as he could. "It was more complicated than that, Emily. I think it probably *always* is. But I know your birth mother made the best decision that she could, and your mother and I are *so* grateful that she did."

Emily didn't want to feel grateful; she wanted to feel sulky. "And I'm supposed to think she's all great and everything?" For not *wanting* her?

Her father shook his head. "No, I think that sometimes you're probably supposed to feel confused, and hurt, and maybe even angry."

That was good, because when it came to this particular subject, she usually felt all three of those things. "And maybe sad, too?" she said.

Her father nodded, looking pretty sad himself.

For that matter, Zack looked sad, too, and when he made a small anxious sound, she reached down to pat him.

"It's not about you and Mom," Emily said quickly, still patting Zack. "It's just when the lady said that, it made me start thinking again, and I felt—well, I don't know. Really *bad*, I guess. But, there really aren't, you know, any answers, are there?"

Her father sighed. "No," he said. "I'm afraid there aren't."

19

When she was getting ready for bed later that night, her mother came into her room. Her expression was so concerned that Emily knew her father must have told her all about their conversation.

"Are you all right?" she asked.

Emily nodded.

"I know I can't do anything about the tourist," her mother said. "But do you want me to speak to Mrs. Griswold?"

Emily shook her head very hard. Because her mother probably *would* stomp right down there and confront her. "No. No, definitely not. She was just *grouchy*, you know?" Mean and intimidating, too, but mostly just—cranky, and unfriendly. "Besides, the other lady bothered me way more, because the whole time, she thought she was being really nice."

"Because it was her first thought," her mother said.

Yeah. Emily nodded. "Like I was the only black person she'd *seen* up here, and that was all that made sense."

Then again, as far as she knew, she *was* the only African-American in Bailey's Cove—or biracial, or whatever it was that she was.

"I can't stand it when you and I are out somewhere together, and people look around for your parents when I'm standing right there," her mother said.

Which happened a lot. Usually, when they were around a bunch of strangers, her mother made a point of standing close by and keeping a hand on her shoulder. Then, before anyone had time to ask any potentially dumb questions, she would say something like "Have you met my daughter, Emily?" And the person would almost look surprised, say, "oh," and then say, "*oh*," when they finally figured it out. If it was any sort of college-sponsored event—where everyone was usually totally into being politically correct, Emily had noticed that people seemed to be faintly disappointed when they saw her father and it turned out that he was Caucasian, instead of African-American. Maybe they thought adoption was less *interesting* somehow.

"You seem to be thinking about all of it a lot

more, recently," her mother said, breaking the silence.

That was true, although she wasn't sure why. Actually, she *thought* about it all the time, but she usually didn't bring it up in conversation. "Maybe because school's starting," Emily said, "and—well, all those new people." People she didn't know who were going to see her as "adopted" first, before they saw her as "Emily."

Or as African-American first, instead of as a person named Emily.

Her mother nodded.

"And—well, another birthday, too," Emily said. "And there won't be any—*anything*, you know?"

No card, or note, or present, or—best of all—*phone call.*

Her mother sighed. "I know. That part is especially hard, isn't it?"

Very hard. And it always hurt her feelings, even though the lack of contact no longer surprised her, year in and year out. She assumed that her birth mother at least *thought* about her, briefly, on her birthday—because it had to be hard to forget having had a baby once. As far as her birth father was concerned, she had no idea, but from what little she had gathered, her sense was that he had never been involved with any of it, and might not even know that she existed.

Which was really weird, if it was true. If he found out, would he be glad—or completely horrified to know that he had had an unwanted child walking around out in the world all of these years?

"Twelve is an especially big one, too," her mother said. "So I think we should really go all out, don't you? With school starting, I don't think any of your cousins could come then, but let's ask Grandma, and Gramps and Grammy to fly in." Which was all of her living grandparents, since her mother's father had died when Emily was seven. "Have a big celebration. And then, they can meet Zack, too. Does that sound fun?"

Emily nodded enthusiastically.

It sounded *very* fun.

The next morning, they took Zachary to the vet for a quick check-up. Dr. Kasanofsky was very pleased with his progress, and his only instructions were to keep doing exactly what they were doing. He also told them—to Emily's delight—that no one anywhere in the *state* had reported losing a white retriever, and that they could probably safely assume that he had, indeed, been a stray.

On the way home, her father went by the town hall so that they could go in and get an official dog license, to go along with Zack's new rabies tag. Zack seemed to like his tags, because when Emily took him for his walk after lunch, he shook his head every so often and the tags would jingle softly together.

Every time they went out, he always seemed to want to walk towards Mrs. Griswold's house—in fact, he veered that way so automatically that she wondered if he might be the dog version of left-handed. It would explain his unerring tendency to want to walk down there. But, since she didn't want to look for trouble, she tried to make a point of steering them in the opposite direction.

Today, the strategy backfired, because as they walked along towards the access road, she could see a familiar figure in a fishing hat pedaling towards them on a black bicycle. It always looked painful when Mrs. Griswold rode, because of whatever was wrong with her legs, and right now, she was also weighed down by three bags of groceries and supplies.

Emily's first thought was to bend down to tie her shoe so she could pretend that she hadn't even seen her. But Zack was wagging his tail happily, so she summoned up her nerve and waved.

162

Mrs. Griswold looked shocked enough that Emily thought she might fall right off the bike, but then she lifted one hand briefly before pedaling harder and continuing past them.

The fact that she had just had a friendly exchange with the meanest person in town was something Emily was probably going to keep to herself.

Emily had never been too sure about whether she liked kayaking, but her mother talked her into going for a short excursion on the sound before sunset, and they had a good time. The water was choppy enough to be interesting, but not so rough that it was scary. They rode in a yellow two-person kayak that was supposed to be really stable—but Emily still almost managed to capsize them when she dropped her paddle and lunged to grab it.

Her father stood on their dock the whole time and took a bunch of pictures. Zack waited next to him, and when they were close enough to the shore, she could hear him whining anxiously and shouted, "It's okay, Zack, we're having fun!"

All of the paddling made her arms tired, and she had no idea how her mother—who was just barely over five feet tall and very thin—did it so effortlessly. She even won races sometimes, and in the den, there was a small shelf filled with her trophies. Emily had never won a trophy that she thought was worth anything, because in her swim class, *everyone* had been given one. She did get a blue ribbon at an art show once, though—and was pretty proud of it. Her parents wanted her to enter more art contests and shows, but she was never sure if her drawings and paintings were good enough, and wasn't sure she wanted to be all competitive about it, anyway. It was more fun just to *draw*, and not worry about what other people thought of her pictures.

Zack still couldn't climb the stairs, although he had started trying—but would whimper and have to be helped back down before he got very far. So she was still sleeping in the den, to keep him company. Since the floor really *was* pretty hard, her mother had started making up the couch every night, and with a little help, Zack could get up there, too, now.

So far, the only one who ever really slept in the homemade dog bed was—Josephine.

Before Emily went to sleep that night, she read three chapters of *Jane Eyre*. Her friend Florence had told her that it was old-fashioned and boring, but so far, Emily liked it a lot—especially compared to *Little Women*, which had kind of annoyed her, because she thought Beth was actually pretty *whiny*.

There were modern books on their reading list, too, but so far, she had mostly been choosing the classic ones. The next book on her list was *Wuthering Heights*.

After giving Zack a biscuit, and Josephine a couple of little chicken-flavored treats, Emily turned off the light and climbed back under the sheet and blankets on the couch.

Once she fell asleep, she had a really bad dream, and couldn't seem to wake herself up.

She was on an old boat, in the middle of the ocean, and it was either dusk or right before dawn. Either way, it was pretty dark, and the seas were rough. The deck was cluttered with coils of rope, piles of nets, line haulers, winches, and a lot of other gear, so that there was almost no room to move around.

The boat was tossing wildly on the waves, and she could smell the strong odor of fish stored in the hold, and rotting bait. Some of the waves were so high that they were washing right over the side of the boat, and she looked for a place to hide. It was hard to keep her footing, and she kept slipping as she scrambled around.

There was dim golden light inside the pilot-house, and she could see two big shapes moving around inside. People? It was hard to see clearly. But, if she could get inside there, she would be sheltered from the waves.

She banged on the door, but they didn't seem to hear her—or they didn't *care* that she was outside, being battered by water and wind. The way the boat was pitching back and forth, she was *sure* she was going to fall overboard, or be swept off the next time a big wave—

Emily woke up, gasping with fear, before realizing that it was only another bad dream. That she was *fine*, and not trapped on some unknown fishing boat.

The couch seemed to be moving, and she saw that Zack was very restless, too—whimpering and shivering in his sleep, with his paws twitching violently.

"Zack," she said, and patted him lightly. "Zack, wake up, boy, it's okay."

He opened his eyes, looking as confused and frightened as she had felt a moment earlier, and she came to a strong—and startling—realization.

It wasn't a bad dream of *hers*. She had just been having *Zack's* nightmare!

20

In the middle of the night, the idea that she and Zack had had the same dream had been really spooky. In the morning, with the sun out and the smell of breakfast floating into the room, it seemed more like something she must have made up. A dream *within* a dream, maybe.

She and her mother spent most of the morning weeding the garden, while her father mumbled something about a very important history journal he was *sure* he had left in his office over at the college—and sensibly escaped from this chore. Emily wished that she could come up with a good excuse, too, but when she tentatively pointed out that she should maybe go do some more reading, so that she would be prepared when school started, her mother just said, "Join the club."

The whole time, Zack lay on the grass nearby, sometimes watching, but mostly napping.

"It still isn't going to grow, is it?" her mother asked, when they were finally finished.

It hadn't so far, so probably not. "It looks much *neater* now," Emily said.

Her mother let out a sigh. "I like to be good at things, Emily."

Emily laughed, since that was a *huge* understatement. No one would ever accuse her mother of putting out a halfway effort on *anything*.

They had homemade onion soup for lunch, which was really good, because they used Vidalia onions, and sautéed them very, very slowly. Then, they toasted slices of French bread in the oven, covered them with Gruyère cheese, and added them to the bowls.

By some strange coincidence—or *not*, her father managed to arrive back home precisely in time to eat with them.

"Took you quite a while to find that journal," her mother said wryly.

Her father nodded, his eyes looking wide, and innocent—and a tiny bit sly—behind his glasses. "I know. It sure did. I really need to straighten that office out, don't I?"

"Well, when it comes time to clean the garage,"

her mother said, "I'm going to misplace a book in *my* office."

If they had a garage-cleaning day, Emily might have to figure out some way to misplace *herself* for a few hours.

After they finished lunch, her father immediately began to do the dishes—which was a smart peace offering. Her mother went upstairs to do some work of her own, and Emily took Zack for a walk.

When they got to the road, he wanted to go left, and she wanted to go right. As usual. But she had no intention of following his lead. For one thing, if he decided to lift his leg or something against Mrs. Griswold's fence, she could already imagine how badly *that* might turn out. So they went right, but he seemed reluctant, and lagged behind her.

"Does your leg hurt?" she asked. "Or your ribs?"

Zack wagged his tail, but didn't pick up his pace.

She started to say something, but then she had this sudden image of Mrs. Griswold, sitting alone in her living room. The only light was coming from the television, and she looked incredibly sad. The image was so vivid that she stopped walking, and tried to figure out why it had popped into her head like that.

The dog looked up at her with great intensity.

Then, he turned around, clumsy with his cast, to head in the other direction.

"No, Zack," she said. "We're not going that way. We're *not*. No way."

He pulled in one direction, and she tugged—gently—in the other. After about a minute, the dog gave in, but instead of carrying his tail high, it sagged down.

She decided to ignore that, but it only worked for about ten steps. She stopped again, putting her hands on her hips. "Zack, I don't want to walk up there. She likes to be left alone, and we really shouldn't bother her."

The dog looked at her, unblinking.

"Well, she *does* like it," Emily said defensively. Because if she didn't, why would she keep to herself for years and years, and go out of her way not to be friendly to people? It had to be an intentional choice, right? "And she doesn't like us, remember? She doesn't like *anyone*."

But now, she had an even *stronger* image of Mrs. Griswold, her expression haunted and lonely, sitting at her kitchen table and staring down at a cup of coffee. It was probably her imagination, but it felt almost as though she was looking at a little private snapshot of her neighbor's life—and it was disturbing.

And it was also disturbing that she didn't know if it was coming from her imagination, or Zack's.

To make it go away, she would just make herself come up with a different image. Emily closed her eyes and pictured them walking by Mrs. Griswold's house. As they passed, Mrs. Griswold came out onto her porch and shouted at them and shook her cane angrily. Then, she even picked up a *rock* and threw it at them.

The dog sat down, cocking his head at her.

Maybe she wasn't concentrating hard enough. Emily made herself re-imagine the scene, with lots of details—the sun, the sound of black flies and seagulls, the smell of wild blueberries and the ocean, the way the dirt road felt under their feet. This time, when she got to the part where Mrs. Griswold threw the rock, she had the stone *hit* her, right in the shoulder, as Zack stood by in horror.

But then, even as she tried to keep the dark pictures in her head, she couldn't shake an answering image of Mrs. Griswold on that same porch, smiling and waving at them. And—crackers. She had a clear vision of—saltines? Graham crackers? Hoarded

Crown Pilots, from before the brand was discontinued, upsetting Mainers everywhere? Anyway, for some reason, she couldn't stop thinking of crackers.

It was pretty unnerving, because the thoughts were so strong and specific, and she couldn't seem to get rid of them.

Also, even though she'd just finished a big lunch, she was suddenly very, very hungry.

Feeling confused—and kind of alarmed by the way her thoughts were jumping all around to weird places, Emily sat down on an old tree stump by the side of the road.

The dog followed her cooperatively, and flopped down in the grass. It must have felt very warm and comfortable down there, because his paws flexed happily and he thumped his tail a couple of times.

This whole situation was just getting too confusing. Was she *really* thinking her dog's thoughts? And was he thinking her thoughts? And were they actually having the exact same nightmares sometimes? Or, was she making all of this up? Was there any way to find out for sure? Because, increasingly, the entire concept was really making her nervous. Either she was reading her dog's mind—or she was crazy.

Or, possibly, both.

"Zack, are we inside each other's heads?" she asked aloud. "Because it feels that way."

The dog rolled playfully in the grass, looking happier than ever.

"Did I have your dream last night?" she asked. "Because—I think I did."

Okay, she *must* be making it up, because he was obviously thinking his own thoughts, and having a very nice time doing it.

Crackers. She kept seeing crackers. On a white plate. All kinds of crackers. *Piles* of them.

She didn't mind crackers, but it wasn't like she was crazy about them. So why couldn't she get them out of her head?

She looked down at Zack, who was still lounging in the grass, just as happy as a clam.

Although, having watched people dig up clams at low tide for *years*, the expression had never made sense to her, because how happy could they really be? Their lives didn't seem particularly interesting, or rewarding.

"Do you like crackers?" she asked him. "Do you *want* crackers?"

Zack looked up at her with the dog version of a big smile.

Was that a yes? It would be a lot easier if he

could *talk*, and she could find out for sure what was going on.

Okay. She would try once more, and then give up for the day. Emily put one hand over her eyes, to try and shut the rest of the world out, and imagined herself standing up, and walking down the road directly towards Mrs. Griswold's house, opening her gate, and walking up to the front door.

There was a jingle of metal tags as Zack scrambled to his feet and strained at the leash, clearly in a hurry to get moving.

She could pretend that wasn't a very clear response—but it would be a lie.

It looked like they were going to have to go walk by Mrs. Griswold's house—*again*.

21

As they walked down the dirt road, Zack ambled along pleasantly, stopping every so often to sniff at bushes and flowers and, once, a turtle, who was sunning itself in the middle of the street. Her dog looked up at her with alarm, and once again, she wasn't sure if *he* was picturing cars racing down the road in a cloud of dust and putting the turtle in danger—or she was.

Either way, that's what she immediately thought.

"Stay here for a minute," she said to Zack, "okay?"

Then, she bent down and picked up the turtle— which was much heavier than she expected. It was also awfully reptilian, the way its legs and head moved, but it didn't try to bite her as she carried it well off the road, into the woods. She decided that the best place would be near a small stream, but behind some big rocks that the turtle might not be willing to climb over to get back to the road. Then, she returned to where Zack was waiting and he wagged his tail.

It *seemed* like he was pleased with her for making sure that the turtle would be safe—but, also, he might just be wagging his tail. Dogs did that, after all. She was just going to have to start accepting the fact that they seemed to be able to understand each other so well—and *enjoy* it, instead of over-analyzing.

Emily slowed down when they got near Mrs. Griswold's house, because she would still much rather turn around and go home. Then, she saw that Mrs. Griswold was sitting in a wicker chair on her porch—pretty close to the exact way she had imagined it—and she felt a little sick to her stomach. But, luckily, their neighbor seemed to be totally involved with reading a newspaper, so maybe they could walk right on by without being noticed, and Zack would be satisfied that she had made the effort.

But Zack stopped and barked a friendly little bark and spoiled *that* plan.

Mrs. Griswold looked up from her newspaper.

"I'm sorry," Emily said quickly. "I didn't expect him to do that. He's usually very quiet."

Mrs. Griswold pursed her lips. "Don't get all in

a tizzy," she said, after a pause. "I daresay he was just being neighborly."

Oh. Had Mrs. Griswold just said the word "*neighborly*"? "Um, yeah," Emily said. "I think he was just saying hi."

"Is it good for him to walk so much every day, all broken up like that?" Mrs. Griswold asked. "It seems to *me* that you're working him too hard."

Was she being accused of being a bad owner? Emily reached down to rest her hand on Zack's head protectively. "We don't go very far. Our vet said that he was really smart, and I should pretty much let him, you know, follow his own instincts. But, he needs to get exercise, to help his lungs heal."

Mrs. Griswold nodded, although her expression was still pretty critical. "Is he hungry? He looks hungry."

It was a safe bet, since he was pretty much always hungry. They weren't supposed to *over*feed him, but sometimes, it was tempting. "Probably," Emily said. "I guess I'll take him home and—"

"Well, it won't do not to keep him fed," Mrs. Griswold said, sounding very stern. "He looks like he's starving."

Did Mrs. Griswold think that they weren't

taking care of him? Emily frowned. "He's just thin. He had lunch, right before we went out."

But Zack was stretching his head out over the gate, and sniffing enthusiastically.

"I don't want him in my yard running willy-nilly, and making a jumble of my flowers," Mrs. Griswold said, her voice rising. "You be sure and always keep him on that leash, you hear me?"

Emily nodded, and tightened her grip on the leather lead. "Yes, ma'am. I mean, no, ma'am. I mean—" She stopped, not quite sure *what* she meant. "Well, that is—"

"Don't ramble like a ninny," Mrs. Griswold said impatiently. "I hear tell that you're a right smart girl. *Act* like it."

Emily couldn't think of a response to that—which probably didn't look very smart at all.

"And why is that animal staring at me so?" Mrs. Griswold asked.

Emily wasn't sure herself, but she followed Zack's gaze until she located an old white china plate on the table next to Mrs. Griswold's chair, which seemed to have a small stack of saltines spread across it.

Crackers.

Naturally.

"I'm sorry," Emily said. "I think he's looking at

your crackers." Maybe her parents were right, and she should really never feed him at the table. "I haven't had time to train him, or—"

"Well," Mrs. Griswold said, and pursed her lips. "Since he's much too thin, I suppose it would be all right if he had one." She hoisted herself up onto her cane, picked up two crackers, and made her way down to the gate. "Is he going to snap them out of my hand?"

Emily sort of wouldn't blame him, if he did, but she shook her head. "No, ma'am. He has good manners."

"Well, we'll see about *that*," Mrs. Griswold said, but held out one of the crackers, and Emily was surprised to see her hand shaking.

Zack gently accepted the treat, crunched it up, and then tilted his head engagingly.

"I suppose he wants the other one, then," Mrs. Griswold said, sounding much more cross than she actually looked at the moment.

Emily nodded. "Yes, ma'am, I think he does."

Mrs. Griswold gave him the other saltine, and after eating it, Zack leaned his head against Mrs. Griswold's arm in a friendly way, and wagged his tail. Mrs. Griswold grimaced—or, just possibly, smiled a little—and gave him a brisk pat.

Looking at the two of them, for the first time, Emily didn't just see a mean, angry lady; she saw what Zack had already sensed—that maybe this was a *lonely* person who, for whatever reasons, really didn't know how to be around other people. "Um, thank you for the crackers," she said. "He liked them."

"Well," Mrs. Griswold said, with a dismissive wave of her hand. "Don't let's make a federal case about it. Off you go now."

Emily nodded—and went. Quickly.

After she got home, she fed Zack again—because he was always hungry. Then, she sat at the kitchen table, drinking some lemonade and watching her mother make a salad to go with the spinach lasagna her father had put in the oven a little while earlier.

"Did Mrs. Griswold used to have a dog?" she asked.

Her mother stopped chopping tomatoes and thought about that. "Yes. They had a little collie mix. I think her name was—Marigold or something. But that was years ago. Why?"

"I don't know. I just wondered." Emily really couldn't imagine Mrs. Griswold naming a dog after a *flower*. Would Zack like it if she had decided to call him "Petunia" or "Buttercup" or something? Very doubtful. "Was she always mean? Like, when you and Dad first moved here?"

Her mother shook her head. "No. I wouldn't say she was *friendly*, really, but it was in that normal Maine way. She used to be very active here in town, but—well, things changed."

Emily had heard so many wild rumors, for as long as she could remember, that she had no idea if any of them were true. "Did she, um, *really* kill her husband?" she asked.

Her mother looked startled, and almost dropped the cutting board. "Why would you ask a terrible thing like *that*?"

That was a much more dramatic reaction than she had expected. Emily shrugged. "I don't know, I just wondered. Want me to set the table? Or, like, make a salad?"

"Emily Roslin Feingold, you are *not* going to avoid the question by offering to be helpful," her mother said, and then paused. "Although, yes, I would appreciate it if you'd peel those carrots, and maybe a cucumber, too."

Emily opened the drawer where they kept the utensils and took out an old vegetable peeler with a wooden handle, which had belonged to her father's grandmother back in, like, the *thirties*—but still worked really well.

"Who told you that?" her mother asked.

Emily shrugged. "Well, people—not just Bobby," she added quickly, "always say so. You know, down at Cyril's and stuff."

Her mother sighed and took a bottle of freshly pressed olive oil and some balsamic vinegar from one of the pantry shelves. "It's a small town, and rumors get started. That doesn't make them true."

Emily had assumed she couldn't be a murderer, or she would be in jail, right? "But, *something* bad happened," she said.

Her mother nodded. "It was right around Christmas—oh, more than ten years ago, because you were tiny. I think they were driving home from a holiday party. But the roads were slippery, and they crashed on that terrible curve right before the big bridge."

Part of Bailey's Cove consisted of small islands, which were connected to the main part of town only by bridges—they were known, respectively, as the big bridge, the little bridge, and the Cribstone Bridge. In some cases, the bridges were only accessible during low tide, and the people who lived on them were stuck, unless they could boat over to the mainland.

"Mr. Peabody heard about the accident on his scanner," her mother went on, "and he and your father went out to see if they could help. You had an ear infection, and were running a fever, so I stayed here with you."

Mrs. Peabody's daughter was a local police officer, and so the Peabodys spent *a lot* of time listening to their scanner, to make sure she was safe.

"So, Mrs. Griswold's husband was, um, you know?" Emily asked awkwardly.

Her mother nodded. "Yes, it was awful. And she was injured, and she's been on that cane ever since. She was driving, so I'm sure she blames herself. She's never been the same."

That made sense. Emily closed her eyes and imagined a terrible winter accident, with Mrs. Griswold being carried into an ambulance and everyone standing nearby looking very grave.

The technique must have worked, because Zack—who was lying on a towel near the back door—sat up straight for a few seconds, before settling down again.

Her mother shook her head. "Sometimes, I would almost swear he was listening to us, wouldn't you?"

This was the perfect moment to tell her mother

all about what she strongly suspected—but Emily found herself feeling shy, and self-conscious. She *wanted* to tell her, but maybe she should wait until she was able to figure it out more clearly.

"Um, yeah," Emily said, and flipped Zack a piece of carrot, which he crunched up. "It really *does* seem that way, doesn't it?"

22

Bobby came over the next day, and they spent most of the afternoon out on the deck, taking turns throwing a tennis ball for Zack to fetch. Emily had known that he was finally starting to feel well enough to play games when he'd pointedly brought a ball to her that morning and dropped it right in her lap.

They got hungry after a while, and went inside to get some cookies and juice—and give Zack a couple of Milk-Bones while they were at it. Josephine appeared in the kitchen at once, and Emily found a couple of tuna cat treats for her.

She hadn't told anyone about some of the things that had been happening lately, and since Bobby was the kind of person who usually had an "okay, whatever, cool" reaction to most things, maybe he would be the ideal person to confide in. So she decided to bring up the subject she had been avoiding with everyone else.

"Do you believe in ESP?" she asked, tentatively.

Bobby shrugged, stuffing another chocolate chip cookie into his mouth. "You mean, reading minds and all that? Yeah. I guess so." He frowned. "Unless it's, like, *fake*."

That wasn't really a helpful answer. "Has it ever happened to you?" Emily asked.

Bobby shrugged again. "Not really. Like, does it count, if the phone rings, and you're pretty sure you know who it is?"

"Not if you have caller ID," Emily said.

Bobby laughed. "And not if you were, like, expecting the call."

That was true, too.

"You know how my mother gets all Irish and superstitious and everything? She totally believes in all that stuff," Bobby said. "She says it runs in families, and—" He stopped.

It was awkwardly quiet for a few seconds.

"Yeah, maybe it runs in my family," Emily said quickly, to try and smooth over the silence.

Bobby looked guilty. "I didn't mean to, you know—"

"It's fine," Emily said. "You *know* it's fine." In fact, it was the sort of thing that happened all the time, and it wasn't a big deal. It might have bothered her a little coming from someone other than Bobby or her parents or other people she knew really well, but even then, it was just the kind of thing people said without thinking. Her cousin Mike was blind, and during a conversation with him, Emily had once said, "See what I mean?" She had felt completely awful about it, but luckily, he had thought it was funny.

It was still too quiet in the room.

"Yeah, I wonder about them," Emily said, finally, "and I wish I knew who they were, and what they're like—but I *have* parents." And traditions, and pieces of history, and all of those things that made a family a *family*. "So, it's really not—just forget it. Anyway, it's the ESP thing I'm worried about."

Bobby looked puzzled. "What, are you, like, reading minds and stuff? Like, can you read *my* mind?"

Emily looked at the door to make sure neither of her parents was listening, especially since her mother had gone out running and might pop in through the back door any minute now. "Promise you won't tell anyone, okay?" she said. "Because it's going to sound strange."

"Hey, cool!" Bobby said. "You *can* read minds? Hey, can you teach me? If I could read *your* mind, I'd never have to study for tests or anything again. I could just, like, *hear* the answers."

Emily shook her head. "No, it's, um—well—*Zack*."

Bobby glanced down at Zack—who was asleep on a beach towel Emily had spread out on the linoleum. "What, you mean, Zack's all psychic and stuff?"

Well—yeah. Kind of. Emily nodded. "I think both of us are."

"Wow," Bobby said, sounding impressed. "That is *wicked* excellent. Like how?"

Where should she begin? "Like when I was dreaming about drowning, he was *actually* drowning," Emily said. "And I felt like I *had* to go outside, even though it was raining like crazy."

Bobby frowned. "Couldn't you have just, you know, *guessed* that, or, like, heard him bark or something?"

"Yeah, that's what I thought," Emily said. "But, it keeps happening, and I don't know—I think it's *real*. I could smell the medicine they were giving him at the vet's office, even though I wasn't in there, I know what food he likes, and the kind of bowl he wanted, and—I don't know if it's really cool, or totally *creepy*."

"Way weird." Bobby frowned again. "Is it scary?"

"Scary" wasn't quite the right word. "It kind of was when I first figured it out," Emily said, "because

I was feeling all this stuff that wasn't even happening to me. Like I really *was* drowning, but I was right there in my room, so it didn't make sense."

"Hunh. He doesn't, you know, *talk* or anything, does he?" Bobby asked. "You know, like E.T.?"

Emily shook her head. "No." Which was good, because then she'd think she was *really* losing it. "He sends me ideas, sort of. Like, I think something I know I wasn't thinking, and then it turns out to be because he's trying to tell me something. I was thinking how mean Mrs. Griswold was, and he was thinking that she needed us to be nice to her, and— it's almost like having an argument, but in *pictures*."

"Wow," Bobby said. "That is wicked freaky."

Emily grinned. "Far out, man."

Bobby nodded in complete seriousness. "Wicked far out. What do your parents think?"

Emily gave him a sheepish look. "I haven't told them yet. I want to be sure it's *not* just coincidences and stuff."

Bobby nodded again and glanced at Zack, who seemed to be half listening, but mostly napping. "Hey, maybe he's an alien! Or an angel, or something! Something all magical, and stuff. Like— parallel dimensions!"

Emily looked at Zack dubiously, and then patted

his head. He wagged his tail, but didn't move otherwise, until she offered him a piece of a cookie, which he gulped down before closing his eyes again. "No, I think he's a dog. A regular dog, I mean. We just—connect, somehow."

"Hunh," Bobby said again, and then grinned. "That is *so* cool. Do you think he was like, *sent* to you or something? Or picked *you* for a reason?"

Bobby was one of her very closest friends in the world—if not *the* closest—so there was no reason not to tell him the truth.

Emily nodded. "Yeah. I don't know what the reason is, or why it's me, but yeah. I *do* think that."

"Wow, you're really lucky," Bobby said, looking very impressed. "Who knows what kind of cool stuff might happen because of all of this?"

Emily nodded. "I know. So far, it's pretty great."

In fact, it might be the best thing that had ever happened to her!

After Bobby's big brother came over to pick him up, Emily went out to the backyard to throw the tennis ball for Zack some more. It seemed as though, even with his cast, he would play for twenty hours straight, but her arm got tired after a while. So they headed back inside to see what was for dinner.

She found her mother sitting at the kitchen table, going over a bunch of bills and other papers.

"Are we going to eat soon?" Emily asked.

"In about an hour," her mother said, sounding distracted. "I'd like to finish this first, and get it out of the way."

Emily shrugged, and opened the refrigerator to find a snack. Despite all of the food she and Bobby had eaten during the afternoon, she was still pretty hungry.

Just as she was opening a peach yogurt, the phone rang.

"I'll get it," Emily said, and her mother nodded without really looking up from what she was doing.

The number was from Oceanside Animal Hospital, and Emily picked up, assuming that they wanted to confirm Zack's next appointment, or something like that.

"Hello?" she asked.

"Hi, Emily," Dr. Kasanofsky said, his voice rather strained. "This is Dr. K. Could I speak to one of your parents for a minute?"

That didn't sound good at all. "What's wrong?" Emily said uneasily. "Is something wrong with one of Zack's tests, or—"

"No," Dr. Kasanofsky said. "It's nothing like

191

that. It's just that—I don't know how to tell you this, but some people just called the office, and—well, they're looking for their dog."

Oh?

Oh.

Oh.

Emily's legs suddenly felt weak, and she had to grab the side of the counter to keep her balance. "I, uh—just a minute." She turned towards the table, covering the receiver with her hand. "Mom, it's Dr. K. He says someone wants *Zack*."

Her mother's eyes widened, and then she quickly got up and took the phone from her.

As Emily listened to her mother's side of the conversation, she started crying. *Hard.*

Zack, who had been noisily drinking water from his dish, trotted over, and Emily sat down on the floor to hug him, crying even harder.

Just as her mother was hanging up, her father came in from the den.

"What's going on?" he asked.

"That was Dr. K.," Emily's mother said, and looked at them miserably. "Zack's owners called to claim him, and they want to come over to Ocean-side tomorrow to pick him up."

23

No matter what her parents did, or said, Emily couldn't stop crying.

It had been days. How could his owners show up, out of nowhere, after *days*? It wasn't fair. It wasn't *right*. It had to be a mistake.

"The people say their dog fell off their fishing boat," her mother told her gently. "And that they tried to save him, but they couldn't. They thought he had drowned."

Emily dragged her sleeve across her eyes. "Why didn't they *look* for him? Didn't they care?"

"I'm sure they tried, Em," her father said. "But, if they thought he had drowned, they—"

"So, they took bad care of him," Emily said bitterly. "If he was on a boat, he should have had a life jacket. He should have had a collar and a license, too. Do they even *love* him?"

Her parents exchanged glances.

"People take care of their pets in different ways," her mother said finally. "We can't judge—"

Oh, yes, they *could*. Emily hugged her dog more tightly. "Well, I'm *not* giving him back. No way."

Her father sighed, and sat down on the floor next to her. "Emily, I know this is awful, but there really isn't anything we can—"

"I'm *not*," she said. "Not ever."

Not to *anyone*.

No matter what.

She spent the next few hours in the den crying, with her arm wrapped tightly around her dog. Zack stayed very close to her the entire time, and the fact that there was no way to explain what was going to happen to him—to both of them!—the next day made things even worse. She did take time to send short, miserable emails to Bobby and a few of her other friends, so that no one would ask her "Hey, how's Zack?" questions ever again, but other than that, she just cried.

And cried. And cried some more.

Her parents came in, together and separately, but she didn't talk to them, and after they kept checking on her endlessly, she turned out the light and huddled on her side on the couch, so that she could pretend to be asleep. She knew they were trying to help her, but right now, she didn't care. All that mattered was that she was going to lose her dog, and there was nothing she could do to stop it.

Crying so much was exhausting, but she never fell asleep. If they were going to take her dog away from her, she didn't want to miss even a second of the time they had left together. Losing him was going to be like losing *herself*, and she couldn't imagine what life would be like without him.

It was just starting to get light out, when she heard a small object smack against the window, and then, a really fake loon call.

Which could only be Bobby.

But, at six in the morning?

She peeked outside through the curtains, and saw him standing down in the yard.

He held a finger to his mouth, then motioned for her to come out.

So she grabbed a hoodie and stepped into her Converse high-tops.

"Shhh," she whispered to Zack, who followed her as she crept softly into the kitchen, and then slipped outside.

"What's going on?" she whispered, walking over to where her friend was waiting for her. "It's really early."

Bobby's hair was all rumpled and uncombed, and he was still wearing the same shirt and jeans he had had on the day before, so she was pretty sure that *he* hadn't slept all night, either.

"Let me take him," Bobby said urgently. "You can tell the people he got lost again, and you don't know where he is. And I won't tell *you* where I take him, so you won't even be lying."

It might be wrong, but it was a *great* idea. It was a *solution*. Even though she was sure they were alone, Emily glanced around to make *sure* that no one was around to hear them. "I don't think we can get away with it."

"Sure we can," Bobby said. "Then, I'll bring him back tomorrow, and you can pretend like you found him."

Even though she really wanted to do it, would the plan even work? "But then, won't the people just come right back?" she asked.

"Maybe, yeah," Bobby said, and frowned. "Okay. So I'll keep him longer. Maybe even a whole week! Or until they stop calling."

She *wished* that would work—wished it with all

of her heart—but she knew it wouldn't. Emily shook her head. "The people might fall for it, but my parents and Dr. K. won't. They'll *make* me give him back to them."

"Maybe," Bobby agreed. "But, it's still worth a try."

It was possibly the only chance she *had* to keep him.

The *only* chance.

But it was wrong.

Not that she cared.

But it was still wrong.

She let out her breath. "We can't, Bobby," she said. "He was their dog, first. I mean, I wouldn't want someone to do that to *me*."

Bobby shrugged. "It's different. *You* take really good care of him. They totally didn't, so he shouldn't be theirs anymore."

Emily suddenly felt more tired and sad than ever, because it occurred to her that *Zack* was adopted, too. It wasn't exactly the same as her situation—but, in a lot of ways, it was. And maybe her parents worried that someday, when they least expected it, *they* were going to get a "We want her back!" phone call. "I know," she said. "But we can't. I wish we could."

It was quiet for a minute.

"Are you sure?" Bobby asked. "I'd totally do it. You *know* I would."

And, at the very least, it might mean that she'd get to have a few extra days with her dog. Zack was leaning against her leg, and she rubbed his ears gently, just the way he liked it.

"I know," she said. "But—I'm sorry. We just can't."

Bobby looked very disappointed, but he nodded.

"But I'm really glad you *wanted* to do it," Emily said.

"We're *friends*, Emily," Bobby said. "I'd always help you."

And, if he ever needed it, she would always help *him*.

Unfortunately, this time, there was nothing either of them could do to make things better.

When she walked back into the house, Zack keeping stride with her the whole way, it took every bit of strength she had not to run outside again and say, "Bobby, I changed my mind, let's do it!" If the people had taken all of this time to look at ads—and hadn't even called the animal shelters to see if anyone had found him, did they *deserve* to have him?

And, when they showed up in a few hours, was

Zack going to be happy to see them, and glad to go? That was almost the worst thought of all.

Her mother was sitting at the kitchen table, with a very serious expression on her face.

"Was that Bobby out there?" she asked.

Obviously, she had looked out the window and seen them together, so Emily nodded. "Yeah. He just came over to say hi."

Her mother made a point of checking the clock. "Early bird."

They both knew that Bobby was notorious for oversleeping—even on his birthday, and Christmas morning.

"Yeah," Emily said.

Her mother got up, poured her a cup of juice, and then gestured for her to join her at the table.

"Hatching up a plan to have Zack conveniently disappear for a while?" her mother asked, once they were both sitting down.

Emily shrugged, avoiding her eyes.

"You could probably pull it off for a few days," her mother said.

Emily nodded. There was no question in her mind that she and Bobby could—and quite easily.

They sat there.

"What did you decide to do?" her mother asked finally.

Wait, did that mean she had *permission* to hide Zack away from the people? Emily checked her mother's expression, and saw that she was just asking for an honest answer. "Nothing. The people would just come back and take him when he showed up again," she said.

"Ah." Her mother nodded. "Would you have done it if you were *sure* you could get away with it?"

Would she? "I'm not sure," Emily said. "Maybe."

Her mother nodded. "Okay, that's honest. I understand why you would want to, but if you did it, how do you think it would make you feel?"

Very, very guilty. "Like I was stealing someone's dog," Emily said quietly, and her mother nodded.

They sat silently at the table for what seemed like a long time. Zack stayed by her side every second, and she patted him nonstop.

"It's awful, and my heart is broken for you," her mother said, "but we always knew that this was a possibility."

Emily nodded. "I thought it was okay, though. Because it had been so long." Almost two weeks, in fact, since the morning she had found him.

"Your father and I thought so, too," her mother said.

She wasn't sure which would be worse—if Zack *did* want to go with them, and leave her, or if he *didn't* want to go with them.

"Is there any way at all I can help?" her mother asked.

Emily shook her head.

All they could do now was wait for the people who were going to come and *take her dog away forever.*

24

They were supposed to go over to Oceanside Animal Hospital at ten-thirty to meet Zack's real owner, who was apparently a man named Mr. McGuire. With every minute that passed, Emily got more and more upset. If it had been her dog—and he *was* her dog!—she would have gotten her parents to drive her over the night before, as soon as she heard that someone had found him. She would never have wanted to wait until the next *day* to see him.

It wasn't fair.

And if Zack had come to her for a *reason*, why was he going to be taken away like this? That wasn't fair, either.

Crying so much was upsetting him, though, and she tried to be brave, for his sake. Maybe he loved her *and* his old owners, and she shouldn't do anything to make him feel unhappy. She should just pat him and hug him and feed him like this was a normal day, so that he wouldn't feel as terrible as she did.

She couldn't stand the thought of eating anything, even though her mother had cooked French toast, topped with strawberries and whipped cream—which would normally have been one of Emily's very favorite breakfasts. Right now, though, the thought of eating made her feel sick.

Zack seemed nervous—probably because he sensed how upset she was—and at about nine-fifteen, he got up and began pacing nervously around the den. He walked back and forth, barely limping, and kept pausing by the windows to sniff outside. Then, he would whine and pace some more.

Emily couldn't bear the thought of taking him on what would be their final walk together—but, if he needed to go out, he needed to go out.

"Okay," she said, and rubbed her sleeve across her eyes, to wipe away the tears that were still falling, as often as not.

Then, out of nowhere, she had the image of an old blue pickup truck rattling along the road—and as she did, Zack began to whine nervously. Then, he stood up on his hind legs with his paws on the windowsill.

His owners. Dogs have amazing senses of smell, and he probably knew, somehow, that his owners were coming to get him.

Zack came over to nudge her leg pointedly, and then ran back to paw at the window screen. He barked—loudly, and then raked his paws across the screen, as though he was going to leap right through it.

Inside, Emily's heart sank. Okay, he did sense his owner. He *recognized* the scent—which meant that he really did belong to someone else.

And that she was about to lose him.

She caught a jolting image of the pickup truck stopping, and then flashes of some men, and—the animal hospital? Yes, she was definitely picturing the animal hospital, and Zack was obviously desperate to get over there, and be reunited with the McGuires, the *real* owners. People he obviously loved—and must have missed so much more than she had ever realized.

"Okay," Emily said, and picked up the bag of food, medicine, toys, and dishes she and her mother had packed earlier, both of them crying the whole time. "It's okay. I understand. Come on, let's go get Mom and Dad."

He was in such a hurry that he beat her out to

the kitchen, and stood at the back door, barking frantically.

Her parents, who had both been sitting unhappily at the table, looked startled.

"What's going on?" her father asked.

"I, um—" Emily swallowed. "I think he wants to leave. I guess—maybe his owners got there early. And—he must love them a lot. So, can we go now?"

Her parents exchanged glances, but quickly agreed, and her father went out to start the car. Zack was urgent and restless during the entire ride over, and Emily wasn't sure why, instead of seeming eager, he seemed—*upset*. Was it because he had missed his owners so much? Or because maybe he was going to miss her, too, and he felt confused?

Maybe he knew how sad *she* was, and so he couldn't relax and enjoy the excitement of seeing his owners again. So it was probably really selfish of her to sit and cry the whole time.

"It's okay if you want to go back with them," she whispered in his ear, since she didn't even want her parents to hear her. "I understand. I just want you to be happy."

Zack leaned back against her for a minute, but then twisted free, and sniffed anxiously at the partially open car window.

It didn't make sense, but she was sensing—anger. Was Zack angry? She found herself picturing Dr. K. and—was *he* angry? *Someone* was definitely angry, but she wasn't sure who it was.

Except, okay, maybe *she* was angry, about having to give him back. But—no, that wasn't it, either.

Emily closed her eyes, feeling such a jumble of images and emotions that she couldn't sort them out. It probably wasn't helping that she was so tired—and sad—but, it was still really confusing.

When they got to the animal hospital, she saw the beat-up blue pickup truck she had pictured. It was parked crookedly near the front door, taking up at least two spots. The cargo bed was full of old fishing gear, and it looked as though the truck hadn't been washed or polished in many, many years.

She didn't want to give Zack back. She didn't want to get out of the *car*. She just wanted to go home—and let Bobby take Zack and hide him for as long as possible.

"Well," her mother said, and let out her breath. "I'm so sorry about all of this, Emily."

She didn't want to walk into the vet's office sobbing, so Emily nodded and wiped her sleeve across her eyes. As she started to open the door, Zack pushed past her with unexpected strength and burst out of the car. Since Emily had been hanging on to his leash, she was pulled right along behind him, and could barely keep up.

Zack ran across the parking lot—cast and all— and banged his paws against the main door. Emily opened it for him—and was shocked when she saw two large men inside, yelling at Dr. Kasanofsky. One of the men even had a baseball bat, and had just broken the screen on one of the computers with it!

Emily stood there, not sure what was going on—or what to say or do.

Dr. Kasanofsky's shirt was ripped, and it looked like his glasses might be broken, too. "Go back outside, Emily!" he said sharply.

The two men turned around, and Emily saw that they looked remarkably alike in baseball caps, faded t-shirts, torn jeans, and work boots. They were probably in their thirties, and neither of them seemed to have shaved recently.

"There he is," one of the men said grimly, and shook his fist at Dr. Kasanofsky. "You *were* trying to hide him from us. I oughta knock your block off!"

"Yup, that's him," the other man said. "Come here, Rocky."

Rocky?

Zack didn't exactly growl, but his lip curled up, and he took several stiff and aggressive steps towards the men.

Dr. Kasanofsky moved quickly, guiding Emily towards the door. "Go outside, please. *Right now*."

And leave Zack and Dr. K. in here alone—with mean men?

"Are they robbers?" she asked.

"*Now*," Dr. Kasanofsky said again, trying to push her outside—just as her parents were on their way in.

"Hey!" her father said, once he got a look at what was happening, his voice sounding deeper than usual. In fact, it was a New York "Don't *mess* with me!" voice. "What's going on here?"

"We've had a little misunderstanding," Dr. Kasanofsky said. "These men thought we might have found their dog. However, I think we can all agree that they were mistaken."

Emily blinked in confusion. What was he talking about?

Everyone stared at everyone else, and Emily's mother broke the silence.

"Emily, go wait in the car," she said.

While the rest of them were in danger, and might get hurt? Emily shook her head firmly. "No way."

"Emily!" her father said.

She ignored him, holding Zack's leash protectively.

"Hey, folks, calm down," one of the strangers said. "We're not about to bother some little girl. I'm Butch, and this here's my brother, Jim." He indicated the man with the baseball bat. "Just give us our dog, that the vet here *stole* from us, and everything'll be okay. Me and my brother'll take him, and go away."

"Okay," Dr. Kasanofsky said pleasantly. "I'm going to need the four thousand dollars for his medical bills, first."

The two men stared at Dr. Kasanofsky—and Emily stared at her parents. Had they really spent *that* much money to help Zack get well?

Jim recovered first. "We're not paying you anything, man. He's our dog, and we're *taking* him."

Zack was supposed to live with people like *that*? If they were really his owners, no wonder he had gotten lost and hurt!

"Oh, I don't think so," Emily's father said, very grim. "No, I don't think so at all."

"Oh, yeah?" Jim took a threatening step towards him. "And who's going to stop us?"

"Well, *I* am, for one," Emily's father said, folding his arms across his chest.

"And so am I," Dr. Kasanofsky said.

Emily's mother nodded. "That makes three of us."

In the meantime, Zack narrowed his eyes and took another stiff-legged step towards the men.

Butch and Jim looked at each other uneasily.

"Yo, we're not looking for any trouble," Butch said. "Just picking up our dog. Come on, Rocky! Time to go home."

The dog promptly turned around, and went to stand directly—and fiercely—in front of Emily, blocking them from being able to get anywhere near her.

The other man, Jim, laughed. "Been spoiling him, haven't you?" he said to Emily's parents. "Rocky, let's go!"

Zack didn't love them. In fact, it was obvious that he didn't even *like* them.

And that they were very, very bad owners—and not nice people, either.

"Oh, and here." Butch dug into his pocket, and

tried to hand her father a crumpled ten-dollar bill. "Take this, for your trouble."

"That doesn't even *begin* to cover the medical bills," Emily's father said, with a very tight smile on his face.

Butch looked uncomfortable, and reached back into his pocket. "Okay. Let's make it twenty."

"Get over here, Rock," Jim said impatiently.

The dog stubbornly stayed right where he was, still not looking at either of the McGuires.

Jim scowled at Emily. "What'd you do to him? That's *our* dog."

Her mother moved her jaw, and then took out her cell phone and punched in three numbers. "Yes, hello," she said into the phone. "Could you please send some officers over to Oceanside Animal Hospital right away? Some people are over here making threats and causing a disturbance." She listened. "Yes, thank you. We'll be right here waiting." Then, she snapped the phone shut. "I think you two had better think about leaving—and *never* coming back."

The McGuires stared pugnaciously at her parents and Dr. Kasanofsky—who stared right back at them.

Then, Jim backed away a few steps, holding up

his hands. "All right, all right, no cops. We were just *talkin'*, man. But we *want* our dog back, got it?"

"Yeah, it's not our fault he got lost," Butch said.

Just then, Emily got a strong image of a storm-tossed boat, and running around frantically, and being caught in something. Something that *hurt*.

"How did he fall off the boat?" she asked.

They all turned as though they had completely forgotten she was still in the room.

"He, um, he just fell," Butch said, unconvincingly.

Except she was sure that *wasn't* what happened. It had been something else. Something bad.

There was a long, tense silence.

"We don't know what happened, okay?" Jim said, sounding defensive now. "We were riding out a storm, and in the morning, when we went out on the deck, he was gone. I think he got caught in the line, or sumpthin'."

So they had left him out alone on the deck all night in the middle of a terrible storm—and Zack had nearly died because of it.

"And now you want him back," Emily's mother said.

Butch scowled at her. "This here's a hunting dog. We use him on the boat, too. You think that's easy to replace? *Of course* we want him back." He coughed. "We're, um, you know, just glad you folks found him. And right thankful."

The last part was so insincere that even Jim looked sort of aghast.

Just then, they all heard the sound of a siren heading towards the building, followed by a second one.

"Decision time, boys," Emily's father said quietly.

Butch and Jim looked at each other.

"Okay. We're gone," Jim said sulkily.

Just as the McGuires started to run out to their truck, the police arrived, and it was noisy and confusing for a few minutes. In the end, Dr. Kasanofsky agreed not to press charges, if the brothers paid for the computer equipment they had broken—and promised never to come anywhere near Bailey's Cove again. Even so, the police officers decided that it would be nice for the McGuires to come down to the station with them and have a little—conversation.

The police officers ushered the brothers outside, and Emily and her parents and Dr. Kasanofsky watched as the two squad cars escorted the pickup truck out of the parking lot.

The McGuires were gone. For good.

And Zack was still *here*, with her.

"Wow," Emily said, and swallowed hard. "I mean—wow."

The rest of them seemed to agree with her.

Emily and her parents helped Dr. Kasanofsky straighten up the office, and made sure that *he* was all right, too.

"I'm fine," he assured them. "They mostly just liked hearing themselves talk." Then, he grinned. "But I'm not sorry you showed up here an hour early!"

Even though there was no rational explanation for it.

"I think Zack could smell them," Emily said uncertainly. "And, well, so we came over right away."

Her parents nodded, although she noticed them exchange uneasy glances for a second.

Once everything at Oceanside was all set, they got in the car to go home. Except for giving Bobby a quick call to tell him the great news, Emily hugged Zack the entire way back to the house, and he never stopped wagging his tail. She also cried a little, and her parents might have cried, too, because they were all so relieved by the way things had turned out.

"Is he really mine?" Emily asked. "I mean, really and truly *mine*?"

Her parents nodded, looking almost as happy and overwhelmed as she felt.

Wow. Zack was *her dog*, and now he always would be. It felt like a miracle.

Once they had pulled into the driveway, Zack leaped out of the car and ran over to the back door. He barked joyfully, and butted his head against it.

Emily's mother laughed. "It looks as though someone is *very* happy to be home."

It sure did.

Emily opened the door for him, and Zack ran into the kitchen, and then, to the bottom of the stairs, still barking. She followed him, not sure what he wanted, except that he seemed to be trying to show her something.

He looked back at her, and then raced up the stairs. *All the way up the stairs!* Without limping!

Wow!

Emily ran up after him, just in time to see him tear into her room and bark playfully at Josephine, who was sleeping on the rug in the sunshine. Josephine hissed at him, and then jumped up onto the windowsill, out of the way, where she began to wash.

Zack immediately galloped out of the room and down the hall, examining the entire second floor in about ten seconds flat. Then, he raced back into Emily's room, his tail wagging wildly. He sniffed at the canvas dog bed on the floor—which she realized he had never seen before. Then, he barked again.

"Are you hungry?" Emily asked. "Maybe I could—"

Before she could even finish the sentence, Zack leaped into the air and landed gracefully up on top of her bed. He wagged his tail some more, turned around in three circles, and flopped down onto the quilt, looking more happy and comfortable than she had ever seen him.

"Good boy," Emily said.

Zack thumped his tail once against the mattress, yawned, and stretched out on his side, taking up most of the bed

Emily smiled, as she watched Zack fall asleep.

Home at last.

ALSO AVAILABLE
FROM SQUARE FISH BOOKS

If you like dogs, you'll love these Square Fish dog books!

Dog Whisperer: The Rescue
Nicholas Edwards
ISBN-13: 978-0-312-36768-8
$6.99 US / $7.99 Can

An adopted girl, an
abandoned dog—together,
they can save others.

How to Steal a Dog
Barbara O'Connor
ISBN-13: 978-0-312-56112-3
$6.99 US / $7.99 Can

Georgina may soon be
homeless, but a missing dog
poster has just given her hope!

Dog Gone
Cynthia Chapman Willis
ISBN-13: 978-0-312-56113-0
$6.99 US / $7.99 Can

When searching for her runaway
dog, young Dill must also
deal with the death of her
mother, and her father's grief.

It Only Looks Easy
Pamela Curtis Swallow
ISBN-13: 978-0-312-56114-7
$6.99 US / $7.99 Can

Do desperate times always call
for desperate measures?

Lunchbox and the Aliens
Bryan W. Fields
ISBN-13: 978-0-312-56115-4
$6.99 US / $7.99 Can

Beware—the fate of the world
rests in the paws of a
basset hound and a pair of
clueless aliens!

Sheep
Valerie Hobbs
ISBN-13: 978-0-312-56116-1
$6.99 US / $7.99 Can

Will this dog ever find a boy or
a place to call home?

SQUARE
FISH

WWW.SQUAREFISHBOOKS.COM
AVAILABLE WHEREVER BOOKS ARE SOLD